THE

BURGLAR

IN

SHORT

ORDER

THE
BURGLAR
IN
SHORT
ORDER

A BERNIE RHODENBARR COLLECTION

BY

LAWRENCE BLOCK

SUBTERRANEAN PRESS 2020

First Edition

ISBN
978-1-59606-957-2

Subterranean Press
PO Box 190106
Burton, MI 48519

subterraneanpress.com

www.lawrenceblock.com
Twitter: @LawrenceBlock

Manufactured in the United States of America

TABLE OF CONTENTS

A BURGLAR'S ORIGINS

O RIGINS ARE DIFFICULT TO pin down. Well, not always. Consider Athena, patron of Athens, invaluable guide to Odysseus, goddess of wisdom, her symbols the owl and the olive tree. As you very likely recall, she sprang full-blown from the head of her father, Zeus.

Now that's pretty clear-cut, isn't it? Bernie Rhodenbarr, the larcenous hero of eleven novels and the shorter works which comprise this volume, emerged from some chamber of myself, but Bernie is no Athena. His entry into the world of fiction may be closer to seepage than to full-blown springing.

So how did he get here?

HIS DEBUT in print, arguably, was in "A Bad Night for Burglars," published in *Ellery Queen's Mystery Magazine* in April, 1977. As best I can recall, I wrote the story the previous September, during a month in Rodanthe, on the North Carolina Outer Banks, where I fished off the pier every day and lived on what I hauled out of the water. (Spot, mostly, but also croaker and skate and, when I was lucky, pompano.)

When I wasn't fishing, I was writing short stories, and this one about a hapless burglar was among them. Most of the others sold to *Alfred Hitchcock's Mystery Magazine*, but my agent sent this one to Fred Dannay at *EQMM*, and early in 1977, shortly after I moved into the Magic Hotel in Hollywood, I learned it had been accepted. It was my first-ever sale to the magazine, and came at a time when I couldn't get much written and couldn't sell much of what I did write, so the news of its acceptance was welcome indeed.

Fred, who with his cousin Manfred Lee constituted "Ellery Queen," never in his capacity as editor met a title he didn't want to change. He published this one as "Gentlemen's Agreement," already widely familiar as the title of a best-selling novel by Laura Z. Hobson, and as soon as I got the opportunity I changed it right back to "A Bad Night for Burglars." That's what it is, and thus it shall remain.

But is the protagonist Bernie Rhodenbarr?

Well, I never called him that. He doesn't really need a name, not in this story, nor does he appear to have one. And it's clear at the story's end that he doesn't have much of a future, either. The likelihood of his return-ing as the titular hero of a whole string of novels would have seemed rather unlikely.

But it's pretty clear to me that he's Bernie. The attitude, the personality—really, who else could he be?

SO THERE I was, ensconced at the Magic Hotel on Hollywood's Franklin Avenue, and a single sale of a short story to Fred Dannay, however wel-come, was not enough to make me solvent. I've written elsewhere of what I'd been going through, and how having spent the past two decades as a free-lance writer left me unqualified for any actual employment. I needed a job and couldn't summon up the grit to apply for one.

Well, that's not entirely true. After I left Rodanthe I landed for a few weeks in Charleston, South Carolina, where one day I responded to a card in a shoe repairman's window. He was looking for an apprentice, and I was addled enough to think this was something I might do. Now 37 is an advanced age for an apprenticeship, and while my fingers could cope with a typewriter keyboard they were hardly agile enough for a cobbler's work, so I'd be hard put to come up with a job for which I was less qualified.

The fellow was set to hire me, but he needed someone who'd stick around, and I figured I'd be leaving Charleston by the end of the month. I could have had a few weeks' work, and earned a few meals, but I didn't have the heart to disappoint the man. He appreciated my honesty, he told me, and had the feeling I had the makings of a damn good shoe repairman—and in the dry and dismal months that followed I wondered if I'd passed up the opportunity of a lifetime.

But I went on drifting, and kept trying to get something written. I was in a motel room outside of Mobile, Alabama, when I wrote what was trying to be the first chapter of a Matthew Scudder novel. In it, an oafish fellow turns up at Scudder's table at Armstrong's. Scudder had arrested him for burglary some years back, and the fellow hadn't learned his lesson, but now the cops were after him for a murder he hadn't committed, and he was on the run and wanted Scudder to find a way to clear him.

Well, it was a premise, but it never got anywhere. I wrote ten or twenty pages, and that was the end of that. It wasn't the first time this sort of thing happened, nor was it the last. Some ideas turn into books; many more turn into landfill.

But those few pages, long since tossed aside and forgotten, gave a name to a character I hadn't yet developed.

BACK TO the Magic Hotel. I couldn't write anything, I couldn't sell anything, and I'd missed my chance in the world of shoe repair. What the hell could I do to turn a buck?

I've written before about the little voice that spoke to me. *"Don't rule out crime,"* it said.

Crime?

"You don't need a résumé," it pointed out, *"or a curriculum vitae. You know how all the job ads say 'Experience a must'? Well, walk into a liquor store and point a gun at the clerk and he's not going to ask you if you've done this before."*

But I didn't want to point a gun at anybody, and I sure as hell didn't want anyone to point a gun at me. Violence? The mere threat of violence? No, I don't think so.

"Burglary," the voice continued. *"Actually, it's a lot like writing. You do all you can to avoid human contact. You set your own hours, and you can work at night if you want."*

And so on.

I thought about it. Seriously? Well, that's hard to say. I did teach myself to use an otherwise useless credit card to breach the door of my hotel room, but I never tried the trick on somebody else's door. So I'd characterize the notion as a fantasy, but a serious fantasy.

Still, who knows where it might have led?

What I do know is where it did lead, to this conversation with the little voice:

"Wait a minute. Suppose I got caught?"

"That's where inexperience is an asset. As a first offender, you might get probation. At worst you'd be sure of a light sentence."

"A prison sentence? Me?"

"How bad would it be? They'd have to feed you. You wouldn't have to worry about coming up with the rent."

"I guess it might not be that terrible, and—wait a minute. Suppose I broke into somebody's house, and the cops came, and I was all set to go quietly, and then—"

"And then what?"

"And then there was a dead body in the other room. Not my doing, but—"

"That would be a problem," said the voice.

A PROBLEM? *A problem?*

The hell you say.

That would be a *book.*

10

AND SO it was, of course. I sat down and wrote a few chapters and a very sketchy outline. While I was proofreading it and wondering what to call it, I saw a phrase I'd written for my narrator's internal monologue. "Burglars can't be choosers," he'd mused, and there was my title. I packed it up and mailed it off to my agent, and he sent it straight off to Lee Wright, the legendary mystery editor at Random House. And, remarkably, she bought it almost immediately, and I worked on it over the summer, and in early fall I finished it in Greenville, South Carolina.

When I'd begun writing, my lead character kept surprising me. The last thing I'd expected was comedy. I'd imagined myself in these unfortunate circumstances, having been caught committing a burglary only to be charged with homicide, and I hadn't seen anything inherently amusing about it. But this fellow, this Bernie Rhodenbarr, while aware of the dire nature of his situation, kept finding humor in it.

This is coming out funny, I thought. I'll have to change it.

"*No, you moron,*" said the little voice. "*Just leave it alone.*"

You think?

"*Definitely. Let Bernie be Bernie.*"

BERNIE.

Bernie Rhodenbarr.

And where did the name come from?

Well, I don't know exactly. I had a sort of shirt-tail cousin whose last name was Rodenberg, and I had always liked the sound of that, but I played with it and liked the look and sound of Rhodenbarr better. But that didn't happen at the Magic Hotel. It happened in that motel outside of Mobile.

That's right. Back in Alabama, where I'd been trying to start a Scudder novel. That guy sitting across the table from Matt had a name, and it was Bernie. He had a last name, too, and it was Rhodenbarr.

And I'd pretty much forgotten about him when I started writing *Burglars Can't Be Choosers,* but I evidently remembered his name, and appropriated it for this new chap, a fellow not at all similar in tone and attitude and worldview to the poor guy in "A Bad Night for Burglars." A fellow, I might add, who had nothing in common with that Alabama klutz aside from his name and his occupation.

IF "A Bad Night for Burglars" was Bernie's debut, although he didn't have a name, and if a previously-aborted Scudder novel named him, then *Burglars Can't Be Choosers* closed the deal. I put that credit card back in my wallet, and before too long I was able to start using it again, but in the manner for which it was intended, opening metaphoric rather than literal doors.

So you could say that Bernie Rhodenbarr saved me from a life of crime.

And if I was off and running, so was Bernie. *Burglars Can't Be Choosers* was published in 1977, and it was followed in short order by *The Burglar in the Closet* (1978) and *The Burglar Who Liked to Quote Kipling* (1979).

It was in *Kipling*, the third book in the series, that Bernie really got his footing. In it he acquired the two defining elements in his life—Barnegat Books, the secondhand bookstore (or antiquarian bookshop, if you prefer) on East Eleventh Street, and, a mere two doors east of the store, Carolyn Kaiser, who grooms dogs at The Poodle Factory, harbors cats in Arbor Court, and who is without question Bernie's Best Friend Forever.

THE BURGLAR *Who Liked to Quote Kipling*, I should note, is the source of two of the pieces in this present volume. A distinguished bookseller in Delaware liked the novel's first chapter, in which Bernie turns the tables on a shoplifter, and arranged to publish it separately in 1980 in an edition of 250 copies, via his imprint Oak Knoll Books. It's now a very collectible item, commanding a strong premium, and it seems reasonable to include it here under the title of the special printing, "Mr. Rhodenbarr, Bookseller, Advises a Young Customer on Seeking a Vocation."

And then, four decades later, the people organizing Bouchercon, the annual mystery convention, began plans for an anthology of Florida-based crime stories, as the 2018 convention was set for St. Petersburg (in Florida, not Russia!). Greg Herren was enlisted to edit the volume and Three Rooms Press signed on to publish it, and Bouchercon official Erin Mitchell wondered if I had a Florida story to contribute.

Well, I had set a whole book in Florida recently (*The Girl with the Deep Blue Eyes*) but if I ever set a short story there, I couldn't think of it. It was Erin's idea to choose the second chapter of *Kipling*, with a Florida reference if not a setting. I agreed, and we decided to call it "The Burglar Who Strove to Go Straight."

The anthology, *Florida Happens*, won an Anthony Award—but the only credit I'll claim for that was that my contribution wasn't sufficiently off-putting to kill the deal altogether. I'm including it here because, well, it *was* published separately...

But I may be getting ahead of myself here.

IN THE late 1970s, what began as an insert in *New York Magazine* had taken shape as *Savvy*, a magazine for executive women. At least one of their editors was a fan of mine, and thought perhaps I could write a story for them—although they had never published any fiction. Their offices were in the Port Authority building on Ninth Avenue in Chelsea, now all these years later the home of Google, and late hours in the office led them to consider what a spooky place it could be after everyone else went home. Was there a story lurking in those unsettling halls? And could I unearth it and write it?

I could and did, and as you'll see it's a third-person story in which Bernie is not the narrator but plays a strong supporting role. They liked it just fine at *Savvy*, and they paid for it, and I kept waiting for it to appear. It was scheduled, I'd be advised, and then it was bumped, and rescheduled, and bumped again. The problem was that *Savvy* was really not a vehicle for fiction, and eventually they realized as much and freed me to publish the story elsewhere.

And various bibliographic sources agree that "Like a Thief in the Night" appeared in the May 1983 edition of *Cosmopolitan*. But I've never been able to confirm this. I don't think it ever appeared in a magazine.

Never mind. It's here now, and has been included in various collections of my work, and a few anthologies.

Savvy, incidentally, limped along until 1991. There have been other unrelated publications with that name, in the US and elsewhere. They haven't published the story either...

THE NEXT Bernie Rhodenbarr short story, "The Burglar Who Dropped in on Elvis," was written during a residency at the Virginia Center for the Creative Arts in 1989. It's a writers and artists colony, and I'd booked a stay there to work on a Scudder novel. I'd come up with a terrific ending, but wasn't sure what it was the ending *of*, and I spent ten days and turned out perhaps 200 pages before realizing that it was not working. I set it aside, and had to figure out what to do with the remainder of my stay at VCCA. Writer colonies are wonderful places to be, but only if you're working on something.

So I began writing short stories, and that worked out really well; I kept coming up with ideas and was able to execute them effectively. One of the stories, "Answers to Soldier," sold to *Playboy* and introduced a character named Keller, about whom I would go on to write half a dozen books. And *Playboy* also snapped up "The Burglar Who Dropped in on Elvis" and published it in their April 1990 issue.

AS YOU can see, "The Burglar Who Smelled Smoke" bears a joint byline—*By Lynne Wood Block and Lawrence Block*. I was invited to contribute to an anthology of collaborative ventures, crime stories jointly written by established writers and their presumably significant others. I mentioned it to Lynne, and said if she could come up with a full-fledged idea, I could do the heavy lifting and turn the idea into a story.

While she was thinking this over, we went for a weekend visit to Otto Penzler's house in Connecticut; he'd had it built fairly recently, and it was a very nice house with an extraordinary library, designed and constructed to house Otto's definitive collection of mystery fiction.

On the train ride home, Lynne rattled off her story idea, complete with an original locked-room murder method. I wrote the story, and the lifting involved wasn't all that heavy. Marty Greenberg took it for his anthology, and I double-dipped by selling magazine rights to the excellent if all too short-lived *Mary Higgins Clark's Mystery Magazine*. It was published in the Summer-Fall issue for 1997.

AND NOW we come to a quintet of occasional pieces, which is to say mini-essays written on one occasion or another, for one publication or another. "The Burglar Who Collected Copernicus" ran in the *Chicago Tribune* in 2000. "A Burglar's-Eye View of Greed" was commissioned by *New York Newsday* in 2002, and subsequently made a second appearance as a limited-edition broadside. "The Burglar on Location" was published in the *New York Daily News*, though I can't determine the precise date. "Five Books I've Read More Than Once" was compiled for the November 2013 issue of *Crimespree Magazine*, while "A Burglar's Complaint" was written at the request of a European publisher for *38 Hours*, a New York guidebook for tourists.

I don't know that any of these brief essays deserve immortality, even that flimsy shadow of it afforded by publication in this volume. They were, I must admit, very easy to write; the approach of interviewing Bernie and letting him natter on is one I seem to find convenient. And they are, let us acknowledge, the very embodiment of ephemera, misty wisps designed to waft away forever when the sun shines upon them.

On the other hand (and doesn't there always seem to be another hand?) Bernie does have a body of followers who make up in enthusiasm what they lack in numbers. They seem to have an unquenchable appetite for more—more novels, more stories, more Bernie.

So I've elected to err on the side of inclusion. They'll bulk up the volume by a few thousand words, and while that may boost production costs a few cents, it won't add anything to the retail price. They're not costing you a penny.

SO THAT'S it?

Well, not quite.

As noted, Bernie's world didn't really define itself until Carolyn Kaiser and Barnegat Books turned up in the third book, *The Burglar Who Liked to Quote Kipling.* There are, to be sure, other continuing elements; Ray Kirschmann, the best cop money can buy, has been Bernie's frenemy from the very beginning.

But it wasn't until the sixth volume, *The Burglar Who Traded Ted Williams,* that he (and we) made the acquaintance of Raffles the Cat.

And high time, too.

You know, some years ago Mystery Writers of America had to address the putative problem that, when it came to reviews and recognition, realistic and tough-minded fiction enjoyed an edge over gentler and more lighthearted books, often known as cozies. Someone proposed splitting the Edgar Allan Poe Award into two awards, for the best novel of each persuasion. (And call one the Edgar and the other the Allan? Never mind.)

There were a lot of things wrong with that idea, but perhaps the strongest argument against it was that you'd have to decide what was hard-boiled and what was cozy, and the gray area was immense. One needed an unequivocal acid test, and I wrote a piece for Mystery Scene proposing exactly that.

There would be two sorts of books, I suggested. Books With Cats and Books Without Cats. No cat and your book was hardboiled, no matter how many recipes and quilt patterns it might include. Toss in a cat and you'd written a cozy, even if the creature turns out to be the Cat from Hell.

But my soft-boiled hero, Bernie, didn't have a cat.

Oh, there were cats in the books. Carolyn had (and still has) two, Archie, who was named after Archie Goodwin, and Ubi, who was not.

"The Burglar Takes a Cat" is an extract from *The Burglar Who Traded Ted Williams* that introduces Raffles—to Bernie and then to all the rest of us. After enough readers had asked me in which book they'd first encountered Raffles, and expressed a desire to relive the experience, I went ahead and ePublished it. It's still available, and readers are still downloading it—so I'm including it here as well.

MOST RECENTLY, Stephen Jay Schwartz invited me to contribute an essay to *Hollywood vs. The Author.* The casting of Whoopi Goldberg as Bernie Rhodenbarr has over the years become a legendary example of Hollywood being Hollywood, and I welcomed the chance to examine the subject in print.

The book, I might add, is quite a collection, with contributions by a host of distinguished novelists and screenwriters, each with a story to tell. James Brown, Max Allan Collins, Michael Connelly, Joshua Corin, Tess Gerritsen, Lee Goldberg, Diana Gould, Naomi Hirahara, Gregg Hurwitz, Alan Jacobson, Peter James, Andrew Kaplan, Jonathan Kellerman, T. Jefferson Parker, Rob Roberge, Stephen Jay Schwartz, Alexandra Sokoloff... I am, as you might imagine, pleased indeed to be in their company.

AND THAT'S it.

Except it isn't, not quite. There's another piece, "A Burglar's Future," written especially for this volume. You'll find it at the end.

A BAD NIGHT
FOR BURGLARS

THE BURGLAR, A SLENDER and clean-cut chap just past thirty, was rifling a drawer in the bedside table when Archer Trebizond slipped into the bedroom. Trebizond's approach was as catfooted as if he himself were the burglar, a situation which was manifestly not the case. The burglar never did hear Trebizond, absorbed as he was in his perusal of the drawer's contents, and at length he sensed the other man's presence as a jungle beast senses the presence of a predator.

The analogy, let it be said, is scarcely accidental.

When the burglar turned his eyes on Archer Trebizond his heart fluttered and fluttered again, first at the mere fact of discovery, then at his own discovery of the gleaming revolver in Trebizond's hand. The revolver was pointed in his direction, and this the burglar found upsetting.

"Darn it all," said the burglar, approximately. "I could have sworn there was nobody home. I phoned, I rang the bell—"

"I just got here," Trebizond said.

"Just my luck. The whole week's been like that. I dented a fender on Tuesday afternoon, overturned my fish tank the night before last. An unbelievable mess all over the carpet, and I lost a mated pair mouthbreeders so rare they don't have a Latin name yet. I'd hate to tell you what I paid for them."

"Hard luck," Trebizond said.

"And yesterday I was putting away a plate of fettuccini and I bit the inside of my mouth. You ever done that? It's murder, and the worst part is you feel so stupid about it. And then you keep biting it over and over again because it sticks out while it's healing. At least I do." The burglar gulped a breath and ran a moist hand over a moister forehead. "And now this," he said.

"This could turn out to be worse than fenders and fish tanks," Trebizond said.

"Don't I know it. You know what I should have done? I should have spent the entire week in bed. I happen to know a safecracker who consults an astrologer before each and every job he pulls. If Jupiter's in the wrong place or Mars is squared with Uranus or something he won't go in. It sounds ridiculous, doesn't it? And yet it's eight years now since anybody put a handcuff on that man. Now who do you know who's gone eight years without getting arrested?"

"I've never been arrested," Trebizond said.

"Well, you're not a crook."

"I'm a businessman."

The burglar thought of something but let it pass. "I'm going to get the name of his astrologer," he said. "That's just what I'm going to do. Just as soon as I get out of here."

"If you get out of here," Trebizond said. "Alive," Trebizond said.

The burglar's jaw trembled just the slightest bit. Trebizond smiled, and from the burglar's point of view Trebizond's smile seemed to enlarge the black hole in the muzzle of the revolver.

"I wish you'd point that thing somewhere else," he said nervously.

"There's nothing else I want to shoot."

"You don't want to shoot me."

"Oh?"

"You don't even want to call the cops," the burglar went on. "It's really not necessary. I'm sure we can work things out between us, two civilized men coming to a civilized agreement. I've some money on me. I'm an openhanded sort and would be pleased to make a small contribution to your favorite charity, whatever it might be. We don't need policemen to intrude into the private affairs of gentlemen."

The burglar studied Trebizond carefully. This little speech had always gone over rather well in the past, especially with men of substance. It was hard to tell how it was going over now, or if it was going over at all. "In any event," he ended somewhat lamely, "you certainly don't want to shoot me."

"Why not?"

"Oh, blood on the carpet, for a starter. Messy, wouldn't you say? Your wife would be upset. Just ask her and she'll tell you shooting me would be a ghastly idea."

"She's not at home. She'll be out for the next hour or so."

"All the same, you might consider her point of view. And shooting me would be illegal, you know. Not to mention immoral."

"Not illegal," Trebizond remarked.

"I beg your pardon?"

"You're a burglar," Trebizond reminded him. "An unlawful intruder on my property. You have broken and entered. You have invaded the sanctity of my home. I can shoot you where you stand and not get so much as a parking ticket for my trouble."

"Of course you can shoot me in self-defense—"

"Are we on Candid Camera?"

"No, but—"

"Is Allen Funt lurking in the shadows?"

"No, but I—"

"In your back pocket. That metal thing. What is it?"

"Just a pry bar."

"Take it out," Trebizond said. "Hand it over. Indeed. A weapon if I ever saw one. I'd state that you attacked me with it and I fired in self-defense. It would be my word against yours, and yours would remain unvoiced since you would be dead. Whom do you suppose the police would believe?"

The burglar said nothing. Trebizond smiled a satisfied smile and put the pry bar in his own pocket. It was a piece of nicely shaped steel and it had a nice heft to it. Trebizond rather liked it.

"Why would you want to kill me?"

"Perhaps I've never killed anyone. Perhaps I'd like to satisfy my curiosity. Or perhaps I got to enjoy killing in the war and have been yearning for another crack at it. There are endless possibilities."

"But—"

"The point is," said Trebizond, "you might be useful to me in that manner. As it is, you're not useful to me at all. And stop hinting about my favorite charity or other euphemisms. I don't want your money. Look about you. I've ample money of my own, that much should be obvious. If I were a poor man you wouldn't have breached my threshold. How much money are you talking about, anyway? A couple of hundred dollars?"

"Five hundred," the burglar said.

"A pittance."

"I suppose. There's more at home but you'd just call that a pittance too, wouldn't you?"

"Undoubtedly." Trebizond shifted the gun to his other hand. "I told you I was a businessman," he said. "Now if there were any way in which you could be more useful to me alive than dead—"

"You're a businessman and I'm a burglar," the burglar said, brightening. "Indeed."

"So I could steal something for you. A painting? A competitor's trade secrets? I'm really very good at what I do, as a matter of fact, although you wouldn't guess it by my performance tonight. I'm not saying I could whisk the Mona Lisa out of the Louvre, but I'm pretty good at your basic hole-and-corner job of everyday burglary. Just give me an assignment and let me show my stuff."

"Hmmmm," said Archer Trebizond.

"Name it and I'll swipe it."

"Hmmmm."

"A car, a mink coat, a diamond bracelet, a Persian carpet, a first edition, bearer bonds, incriminating evidence, eighteen-and-a-half minutes of tape—"

"What was that last?"

"Just my little joke," said the burglar. "A coin collection, a stamp collection, psychiatric records, phonograph records, police records—"

"I get the point."

"I tend to prattle when I'm nervous."

"I've noticed."

"If you could point that thing elsewhere—"

Trebizond looked down at the gun in his hand. The gun continued to point at the burglar.

"No," Trebizond said, with evident sadness. "No, I'm afraid it won't work."

"Why not?"

"In the first place, there's nothing I really need or want. Could you steal me a woman's heart? Hardly. And more to the point, how could I trust you?"

"You could trust me," the burglar said. "You have my word on that."

"My point exactly. I'd have to take your word that your word is good, and where does that lead us? Down the proverbial garden path, I'm afraid. No, once I let you out from under my roof I've lost my advantage. Even if I have a gun trained on you, once you're in the open I can't shoot you with impunity. So I'm afraid—"

"No!"

Trebizond shrugged. "Well, really," he said. "What use are you? What are you good for besides being killed? Can you do anything besides steal, sir?"

"I can make license plates."

"Hardly a valuable talent."

"I know," said the burglar sadly. "I've often wondered why the state bothered to teach me such a pointless trade. There's not even much call for counterfeit license plates, and they've got a monopoly on making the legitimate ones. What else can I do? I must be able to do something. I could shine your shoes, I could polish your car—"

"What do you do when you're not stealing?"

"Hang around," said the burglar. "Go out with ladies. Feed my fish, when they're not all over my rug. Drive my car when I'm not mangling its fenders. Play a few games of chess, drink a can or two of beer, make myself a sandwich—"

"Are you any good?"

"At making sandwiches?"

"At chess."

"I'm not bad."

"I'm serious about this."

"I believe you are," the burglar said. "I'm not your average woodpusher, if that's what you want to know. I know the openings and I have a good sense of space. I don't have the patience for tournament play, but at the chess club downtown I win more games than I lose."

"You play at the club downtown?"

"Of course. I can't burgle seven nights a week, you know. Who could stand the pressure?"

"Then you can be of use to me," Trebizond said.

"You want to learn the game?"

"I know the game. I want you to play chess with me for an hour until my wife gets home. I'm bored, there's nothing in the house to read, I've never cared much for television, and it's hard for me to find an interesting opponent at the chess table."

"So you'll spare my life in order to play chess with me."

"That's right."

"Let me get this straight," the burglar said. "There's no catch to this, is there? I don't get shot if I lose the game or anything tricky like that, I hope."

"Certainly not. Chess is a game that ought to be above gimmickry."

"I couldn't agree more," said the burglar. He sighed a long sigh. "If I didn't play chess," he said, "you wouldn't have shot me, would you?"

"It's a question that occupies the mind, isn't it?"

"It is," said the burglar.

THEY PLAYED in the front room. The burglar drew the white pieces in the first game, opened King's Pawn, and played what turned out to be a reasonably imaginative version of the Ruy Lopez. At the sixteenth move Trebizond forced the exchange of knight for rook, and not too long afterward the burglar resigned.

In the second game the burglar played the black pieces and offered the Sicilian Defense. He played a variation that Trebizond wasn't familiar with. The game stayed remarkably even until in the end game the burglar succeeded in developing a passed pawn. When it was clear he would be able to queen it, Trebizond tipped over his king, resigning.

"Nice game," the burglar offered.

"You play well."

"Thank you."

"Seems a pity that—"

His voice trailed off. The burglar shot him an inquiring look. "That I'm wasting myself as a common criminal? Is that what you were going to say?"

"Let it go," Trebizond said. "It doesn't matter."

They began setting up the pieces for the third game when a key slipped into a lock. The lock turned, the door opened, and Melissa Trebizond stepped into the foyer and through it to the living room. Both got to their feet. Mrs. Trebizond advanced, a vacant smile on her pretty face. "You found a new friend to play chess with," she said. "I'm happy for you."

Trebizond set his jaw. From his back pocket he drew the burglar's pry bar. It had an even nicer heft than he had thought. "Melissa," he said, "I've no need to waste time with a recital of your sins. No doubt you know precisely why you deserve this."

She stared at him, obviously not having understood a word he had said to her, whereupon Archer Trebizond brought the pry bar down on the top of her skull. The first blow sent her to her knees. Quickly he struck her three more times, wielding the metal bar with all his strength, then turned to look into the wide eyes of the burglar.

"You've killed her," the burglar said.

"Nonsense," said Trebizond, taking the bright revolver from his pocket once again.

"Isn't she dead?"

"I hope and pray she is," Trebizond said, "but I haven't killed her. You've killed her."

"I don't understand."

"The police will understand," Trebizond said, and shot the burglar in the shoulder. Then he fired again, more satisfactorily this time, and the burglar sank to the floor with a hole in his heart.

Trebizond scooped the chess pieces into their box, swept up the board, and set about the business of arranging things. He suppressed an urge to whistle. He was, he decided, quite pleased with himself. Nothing was ever entirely useless, not to a man of resources. If fate sent you a lemon, you made lemonade.

MR. RHODENBARR, BOOKSELLER, ADVISES A YOUNG CUSTOMER ON SEEKING A VOCATION

I SUPPOSE HE MUST have been in his early twenties. It was hard to be sure of his age because there was so little of his face available for study. His red-brown beard began just below his eyes, which in turn lurked behind thick-lensed horn-rims. He wore a khaki army shirt, unbuttoned, and beneath it his T-shirt advertised the year's fashionable beer, a South Dakota brand reputedly brewed with organic water. His pants were brown corduroy, his running shoes blue with a gold stripe. He was toting a Braniff Airlines flight bag in one ill-manicured hand and the Everyman's Library edition of *The Poems of William Cowper* in the other.

He set the book down next to the cash register, reached into a pocket, found two quarters, and placed them on the counter alongside the book.

"Ah, poor Cowper," I said, picking up the book. Its binding was shaky, which was why it had found its way to my bargain table. "My favorite's 'The Retired Cat.' I'm pretty sure it's in this edition." He shifted his weight from foot to foot while I scanned the table of contents. "Here it is. Page one-fifty. You know the poem?"

"I don't think so."

"You'll love it. The bargain books are forty cents or three for a dollar, which is even more of a bargain. You just want the one?"

"That's right." He pushed the two quarters an inch or so closer to me. "Just the one."

"Fine," I said. I looked at his face. All I could really see was his brow, and it looked untroubled, and I would have to do something about that. "Forty cents for the Cowper, and three cents for the Governor in Albany, mustn't forget him, and what does that come to?" I leaned over the counter and dazzled him with my pearly-whites. "I make it thirty-two dollars and seventy cents," I said.

"Huh?"

"That copy of Byron. Full morocco marbled endpapers, and I believe it's marked fifteen dollars. The Wallace Stevens is a first edition and it's a bargain at twelve. The novel you took was only three dollars or so, and I suppose you just wanted to read it because you couldn't get anything much reselling it."

"I don't know what you're talking about."

I moved out from behind the counter, positioning myself between him and the door. He didn't look as though he intended to sprint but he was wearing running shoes and you never can tell. Thieves are an unpredictable lot.

"In the flight bag," I said. "I assume you'll want to pay for what you took."

"This?" He looked down at the flight bag as if astonished to find it dangling from his fingers. "This is just my gym stuff. You know—sweat socks, a towel, like that."

"Suppose you open it."

Perspiration was beading on his forehead but he was trying to tough it out. "You can't make me," he said. "You've got no authority."

"I can call a policeman. He can't make you open it, either, but he can walk you over to the station house and book you, and *then* he can open it, and do you really want that to happen? Open the bag."

He opened the bag. It contained sweat socks, a towel, a pair of lemon-yellow gym shorts, and the three books I had mentioned along with a nice clean first edition of Steinbeck's *The Wayward Bus,* complete with dust wrapper. It was marked $17.50, which seemed a teensy bit high.

"I didn't get that here," he said.

"You have a bill of sale for it?"

"No, but—"

I scribbled briefly, then gave him another smile. "Let's call it fifty dollars even," I said, "and let's have it."

"You're charging me for the Steinbeck?"

"Uh-huh."

"But I had it with me when I came in."

"Fifty dollars," I said.

"Look, I don't want to *buy* these books." He rolled his eyes at the ceiling. "Oh God, why did I have to come in here in the first place? Look, I don't want any trouble."

"Neither do I."

"And the last thing I want is to buy anything. Look, keep the books, keep the Steinbeck too, the hell with it. Just let me get out of here, huh?"

"I think you should buy the books."

"I don't have the money. I got fifty cents. Look, keep the fifty cents too, okay? Keep the shorts and the towel, keep the sweat socks, okay? Just let me get the hell out of here, okay?"

"You don't have any money?"

"No, nothing. Just the fifty cents. Look—"

"Let's see your wallet."

"What are you—I don't have a wallet."

"Right hip pocket. Take it out and hand it to me."

"I don't believe this is happening."

I snapped my fingers. "The wallet."

It was a nice enough black pinseal billfold, complete with the telltale outline of a rolled condom to recall my own lost adolescence. There was almost a hundred dollars in the currency compartment. I counted out fifty dollars in fives and tens, replaced the rest, and returned the wallet to its owner.

"That's my money," he said.

"You just bought books with it," I told him. "Want a receipt?"

"I don't even want the books, dammit." His eyes were watering behind the thick glasses. "What am I going to do with them, anyway?"

"I suppose reading them is out. What did you plan to do with them originally?"

He stared at his track shoes. "I was going to sell them."

"To whom?"

"I don't know. Some store."

"How much were you going to get for them?"

"I don't know. Fifteen, twenty dollars."

"You'd wind up taking ten."

"I suppose so."

"Fine," I said. I peeled off one of his tens and pressed it into his palm. "Sell them to me."

"Huh?"

"Saves running from store to store. I can use good books, they're the very sort of item I stock, so why not take the ten dollars from me?"

"This is crazy," he said.

"Do you want the books or the money? It's up to you."

"I don't want the books."

"Do you want the money?"

"I guess so."

I took the books from him and stacked them on the counter. "Then put it in your wallet," I said, "before you lose it."

"This is the craziest thing ever. You took fifty bucks from me for books I didn't want and now you're giving me ten back. I'm out forty dollars, for God's sake."

"Well, you bought high and sold low. Most people try to work it the other way around."

"*I* should call a cop. I'm the one getting robbed."

I packed his gym gear into the Braniff bag, zipped it shut, handed it to him. Then I extended a forefinger and chucked him under his hairy chin.

"A tip," I said.

"Huh?"

"Get out of the business."

He looked at me.

"Find another line of work. Quit lifting things. You're not terribly good at it and I'm afraid you're temperamentally unsuited to the life that goes with it. Are you in college?"

"I dropped out."

"Why?"

"It wasn't relevant."

"Few things are, but why don't you see if you can't get back in? Pick up a diploma and find some sort of career that suits you. You're not cut out to be a professional thief."

"A professional—" He rolled his eyes again. "Jesus, I ripped off a couple of books. Don't make a life's work out of it, huh?"

"Anybody who steals things for resale is a professional criminal," I told him. "You just weren't doing it in a very professional manner, that's all. But I'm serious about this. Get out of the business." I laid a hand lightly on his wrist. "Don't take this the wrong way," I said, "but the thing is you're too dumb to steal."

THE BURGLAR
WHO STROVE
TO GO STRAIGHT

AFTER HE'D LEFT I tucked his forty dollars into my wallet, where it promptly became *my* forty dollars. I marked the Steinbeck down to fifteen dollars before shelving it and its companions. While doing this I spotted a few errant volumes and put them back where they belonged.

Browsers came and went. I made a few sales from the bargain table, then moved a Heritage Club edition of Virgil's *Eclogues* (boxed, the box water-damaged, slight rubbing on spine, price $8.50). The woman who bought the Virgil was a little shopworn herself, with a blocky figure and a lot of curly orange hair. I'd seen her before but this was the first time she'd bought anything, so things were looking up.

I watched her carry Virgil home, then settled in behind the counter with a Grosset & Dunlap reprint of *Soldiers Three*. I'd been working my way through my limited stock of Kipling lately. Some of the books were ones I'd read years ago, but I was reading *Soldiers Three* for the first time and really enjoying my acquaintance with Ortheris and Learoyd and Mulvaney when the little bells above my door tinkled to announce a visitor.

I looked up to see a man in a blue uniform lumbering across the floor toward me. He had a broad, open, honest face, but in my new trade one learned quickly not to judge a book by its cover. My visitor was Ray Kirschmann, the best cop money could buy, and money could buy him seven days a week.

"Hey, Bern," he said, and propped an elbow on the counter. "Read any good books lately?"

"Hello, Ray."

"Watcha readin'?" I showed him. "Garbage," he said. "A whole store full of books, you oughta read somethin' decent."

"What's decent?"

"Oh, Joseph Wambaugh, Ed McBain. Somebody who tells it straight."

"I'll keep it in mind."

"How's business?"

"Not too bad, Ray."

"You just sit here, buy books, sell books, and you make a livin'. Right?"

"It's the American way."

"Uh-huh. Quite a switch for you, isn't it?"

"Well, I like working days, Ray."

"A whole career change, I mean. Burglar to bookseller. You know what that sounds like? A title. You could write a book about it. *From Burglar to Bookseller.* Mind a question, Bernie?"

And what if I did? "No," I said.

"What the hell do you know about books?"

"Well, I was always a big reader."

"In the jug, you mean."

"Even on the outside, all the way back to childhood. You know what Emily Dickinson said. 'There is no frigate like a book.'"

"Frig it is right. You didn't just run around buyin' books and then open up a store."

"The store was already here. I was a customer over the years, and I knew the owner and he wanted to sell out and go to Florida."

"And right now he's soakin' up the rays."

"As a matter of fact, I heard he opened up another store in St. Petersburg. Couldn't take the inactivity."

"Well, good for him. How'd you happen to come up with the scratch to buy this place, Bernie?"

"I came into a few dollars."

"Uh-huh. A relative died, somethin' like that."

"Something like that."

"Right. What I figure, you dropped out of sight for a month or so during the winter. January, wasn't it?"

"And part of February."

"I figure you were down in Florida doin' what you do best, and you hit it pretty good and walked with a short ton of jewelry. I figure you wound up with a big piece of change and decided Mrs. Rhodenbarr's boy Bernard oughta fix hisself up with a decent front."

"That's what you figure, Ray?"

"Uh-huh."

I thought for a minute. "It wasn't Florida," I said.

"Nassau, then. St. Thomas. What the hell."

"Actually, it was California. Orange County."

"Same difference."

"And it wasn't jewels. It was a coin collection."

"You always went for them things."

"Well, they're a terrific investment."

"Not with you on the loose they aren't. You made out like a bandit on the coins, huh?"

"Let's say I came out ahead."

"And bought this place."

"That's right. Mr. Litzauer didn't want a fortune for it. He set a fair price for the inventory and threw in the fixtures and the good will."

"Barnegat Books. Where'd you get the name?"

"I kept it. I didn't want to have to spring for a new sign. Litzauer had a summer place at Barnegat Light on the Jersey shore. There's a lighthouse on the sign."

"I didn't notice. You could call it Burglar Books. 'These books are a steal'—there's your slogan. Get it?"

"I'm sure I will sooner or later."

"Hey, are you gettin' steamed? I didn't mean nothin' by it. It's a nice front, Bern. It really is."

"It's not a front. It's what I do."

"Huh?"

"It's what I do for a living, Ray, and it's *all* I do for a living. I'm in the book business."

"Sure you are."

"I'm serious about this."

"Serious. Right."

"I am."

"Uh-huh. Listen, the reason I dropped in, I was thinkin' about you just the other day. What it was, my wife was gettin' on my back. You ever been married?"

"No."

"You're so busy gettin' settled, maybe marriage is the next step. Nothin' like it for settlin' a man. What she wanted, here it's October already and she's expectin' a long winter. You never met my wife, did you?"

"I talked to her on the phone once."

"'The leaves are turnin' early, Ray. That means a cold winter.' That's what she tells me. If the trees don't turn until late, then *that* means a cold winter."

"She likes it cold?"

"What she likes is if it's cold and she's warm. What she's drivin' at is a fur coat."

"Oh."

"She goes about five-six, wears a size-sixteen dress. Sometimes she diets down to a twelve, sometimes she packs in the pasta and gets up to an eighteen. Fur coats, I don't figure they got to fit like gloves anyway, right?"

"I don't know much about them."

"What she wants is mink. No wild furs or endangered species because she's a fanatic on the subject. Minks, see, they grow the little bastards on these ranches, so there's none of that sufferin' in traps, and the animal's not endangered or any of that stuff. All that they do is they gas 'em and skin 'em out."

"How nice for the minks. It must be like going to the dentist."

"Far as the color, I'd say she's not gonna be too fussy. Just so it's one of your up-to-date colors. Your platinum, your champagne. Not the old dark-brown shades."

I nodded, conjuring up an image of Mrs. Kirschmann draped in fur. I didn't know what she looked like, so I allowed myself to picture a sort of stout Edith Bunker.

"Oh," I said suddenly. "There's a reason you're telling me this."

"Well, I was thinkin', Bern."

"I'm out of the business, Ray."

"What I was thinkin', you might run into a coat in the course of things, know what I mean? I was thinkin' that you and me, we go back a ways, we been through a lot, the two of us, and—"

"I'm not a burglar anymore, Ray."

"I wasn't countin' on a freebie, Bernie. Just a bargain."

"I don't steal anymore, Ray."

"I hear you talkin', Bern."

"I'm not as young as I used to be. Nobody ever is but these days I'm starting to feel it. When you're young nothing scares you. When you get older everything does. I don't ever want to go inside again, Ray. I don't like prisons."

"These days they're country clubs."

"Then they changed a whole hell of a lot in the past few years, because I swear I never cared for them myself. You meet a better class of people on the D train."

"Guy like you, you could get a nice job in the prison library."

"They still lock you in at night."

"So you're straight, right?"

"That's right."

"I been here how long? All that time you haven't had a single person walk in the store."

"Maybe the uniform keeps 'em away, Ray."

"Maybe business ain't what it might be. You been in the business how long, Bern? Six months?"

"Closer to seven."

"Bet you don't even make the rent."

"I do all right." I marked my place in *Soldiers Three,* closed the book, put it on the shelf behind the counter. "I made a forty-dollar profit from one customer earlier this afternoon and I swear it was easier than stealing."

"Is that a fact. You're a guy made twenty grand in an hour and a half when things fell right."

"And went to jail when they didn't."

"Forty bucks. I can see where that'd really have you turning handsprings."

"There's a difference between honest money and the other kind."

"Yeah, and the difference comes to somethin' like $19,960. This here, Bern, this is nickels and dimes. Let's be honest. You can't live on this."

"I never stole that much, Ray. I never lived that high. I got a small apartment on the Upper West Side, I stay out of night clubs, I do my own wash in the machines in the basement. The store's steady. You want to give me a hand with this?"

He helped me drag the bargain table in from the sidewalk. He said, "Look at this. A cop and a burglar both doin' physical work. Somebody should take a picture. What do you get for these? Forty cents, three for a buck? And that's keepin' you in shirts and socks, huh?"

"I'm a careful shopper."

"Look, Bern, if there's some reason you don't wanna help me out on this coat thing—"

"Cops," I said.

"What about cops?"

"A guy rehabilitates himself and you refuse to believe it. You talk yourselves hoarse telling me to go straight—"

"When the hell did I ever tell you to go straight? You're a first-class burglar. Why would I tell you to change?"

He let go of it while I filled a shopping bag with hardcover mysteries and began shutting down for the night. He told me about his partner, a clean-cut and soft-spoken young fellow with a fondness for horses and a wee amphetamine habit.

"All he does is lose and bitch about it," Ray complained, "until this past week when he starts pickin' the ponies with x-ray vision. Now all he does is win, and I swear I liked him better when he was losin'."

"His luck can't last forever, Ray."

"That's what I been tellin' myself. What's that, steel gates across the windows? You don't take chances, do you?"

I drew the gates shut, locked them. "Well, they were already here," I said stiffly. "Seems silly not to use them."

"No sense makin' it easy for another burglar, huh? No honor among thieves, isn't that what they say? What happens if you forget the key, huh, Bern?"

He didn't get an answer, nor do I suppose he expected one. He chuckled instead and laid a heavy hand on my shoulder. "I guess you'd just call a locksmith," he said. "You couldn't pick the lock, not bein' a burglar anymore. All you are is a guy who sells books."

LIKE A THIEF
IN THE NIGHT

AT 11:30 THE TELEVISION anchorman counseled her to stay tuned for the late show, a vintage Hitchcock film starring Cary Grant. For a moment she was tempted. Then she crossed the room and switched off the set.

There was a last cup of coffee in the pot. She poured it and stood at the window with it, a tall and slender woman, attractive, dressed in the suit and silk blouse she'd worn that day at the office. A woman who could look at once efficient and elegant, and who stood now sipping black coffee from a bone-china cup and gazing south and west.

Her apartment was on the twenty-second floor of a building located at the corner of Lexington Avenue and Seventy-sixth Street, and her vista was quite spectacular. A midtown skyscraper blocked her view of the building where Tavistock Corp. did its business, but she fancied she could see right through it with x-ray vision.

The cleaning crew would be finishing up now, she knew, returning their mops and buckets to the cupboards and changing into street clothes, preparing to go off-shift at midnight. They would leave a couple of lights on in Tavistock's seventeenth floor suite as well as elsewhere throughout the building. And the halls would remain lighted, and here and there in the building someone would be working all night, and—

She liked Hitchcock movies, especially the early ones, and she was in love with Cary Grant. But she also liked good clothes and bone-china cups and the view from her apartment and the comfortable, well-appointed apartment itself. And so she rinsed the cup in the sink and put on a coat and took the elevator to the lobby, where the florid-faced doorman made a great show of hailing her a cab.

There would be other nights, and other movies.

THE TAXI dropped her in front of an office building in the West Thirties. She pushed through the revolving door and her footsteps on the marble floor sounded impossibly loud to her. The security guard, seated at a small table by the bank of elevators, looked up from his magazine at her approach. She said, "Hello, Eddie," and gave him a quick smile.

"Hey, how ya doin'," he said, and she bent to sign herself in as his attention returned to his magazine. In the appropriate spaces she scribbled *Elaine Halder, Tavistock, 1704,* and, after a glance at her watch, *12:15.*

She got into a waiting elevator and the doors closed without a sound.

She'd be alone up there, she thought. She'd glanced at the record sheet while signing it, and no one had signed in for Tavistock or any other office on seventeen.

Well, she wouldn't be long.

When the elevator doors opened she stepped out and stood for a moment in the corridor, getting her bearings. She took a key from her purse and stared at it for a moment as if it were an artifact from some unfamiliar civilization. Then she turned and began walking the length of the freshly mopped corridor, hearing nothing but the echo of her boisterous footsteps.

1704. An oak door, a square of frosted glass, unmarked but for the suite number and the name of the company. She took another thoughtful glance at the key before fitting it carefully into the lock.

It turned easily. She pushed the door inward and stepped inside, letting the door swing shut behind her.

And gasped.

There was a man not a dozen yards from her.

"HELLO," HE said.

He was standing beside a rosewood-topped desk, the center drawer of which was open, and there was a spark in his eyes and a tentative smile on his lips. He was wearing a gray suit patterned in a windowpane check. His shirt collar was buttoned down, his narrow tie neatly knotted. He was two or three years older than she, she supposed, and perhaps that many inches taller.

Her hand was pressed to her breast, as if to still a pounding heart. But her heart wasn't really pounding. She managed a smile. "You startled me," she said. "I didn't know anyone would be here."

"We're even."

"I beg your pardon?"

"I wasn't expecting company."

He had nice white even teeth, she noticed. She was apt to notice teeth. And he had an open and friendly face, which was also something she was inclined to notice, and why was she suddenly thinking of Cary Grant? The movie she hadn't seen, of course, that plus this Hollywood meet-cute opening, with the two of them encountering each other unexpectedly in this silent tomb of an office, and—

And he was wearing rubber gloves.

Her face must have registered something because he frowned, puzzled. Then he raised his hands and flexed his fingers. "Oh, these," he said. "Would it help if I spoke of an eczema brought on by exposure to the night air?"

"There's a lot of that going around."

"I knew you'd understand."

"You're a prowler."

"The word has the nastiest connotations," he objected. "One imagines a lot of lurking in shrubbery. There's no shrubbery here beyond the odd rubber plant and I wouldn't lurk in it if there were."

"A thief, then."

"A thief, yes. More specifically, a burglar. I might have stripped the gloves off when you stuck your key in the lock but I'd been so busy listening to your footsteps and hoping they'd lead to another office that I quite forgot I was wearing these things. Not that it would have made much difference. Another minute and you'd have realized that you've never set eyes on me before, and at that point you'd have wondered what I was doing here."

"What are you doing here?"

"My kid brother needs an operation."

"I thought that might be it. Surgery for his eczema."

He nodded. "Without it he'll never play the trumpet again. May I be permitted an observation?"

"I don't see why not."

"I observe that you're afraid of me."

"And here I thought I was doing such a super job of hiding it."

"You were, but I'm an incredibly perceptive human being. You're afraid I'll do something violent, that he who is capable of theft is equally capable of mayhem."

"Are you?"

"Not even in fantasy. I'm your basic pacifist. When I was a kid my favorite book was *Ferdinand the Bull*."

"I remember him. He didn't want to fight. He just wanted to smell the flowers."

"Can you blame him?" He smiled again, and the adverb that came to her was *disarmingly*. More like Alan Alda than Cary Grant, she decided. Well, that was all right. There was nothing wrong with Alan Alda.

"You're afraid of *me,"* she said suddenly.

"How'd you figure that? A slight quiver in the old upper lip?"

"No. It just came to me. But why? What could I do to you?"

"You could call the, uh, cops."

"I wouldn't do that."

"And I wouldn't hurt you."

"I know you wouldn't."

"Well," he said, and sighed theatrically. "Aren't you glad we got all that out of the way?"

SHE WAS, rather. It was good to know that neither of them had any-thing to fear from the other. As if in recognition of this change in their relationship she took off her coat and hung it on the pipe rack, where a checked topcoat was already hanging. His, she assumed. How readily he made himself at home!

She turned to find he was making himself further at home, rummag-ing deliberately in the drawers of the desk. What cheek, she thought, and felt herself beginning to smile.

She asked him what he was doing.

"Foraging," he said, then drew himself up sharply. "This isn't your desk, is it?"

"No."

"Thank heaven for that."

"What were you looking for, anyway?"

He thought for a moment, then shook his head. "Nope," he said. "You'd think I could come up with a decent story but I can't. I'm looking for some-thing to steal."

"Nothing specific?"

"I like to keep an open mind. I didn't come here to cart off the IBM Selectrics. But you'd be surprised how many people leave cash in their desks."

"And you just take what you find?"

He hung his head. "I know," he said. "It's a moral failing. You don't have to tell me."

"Do people really leave cash in an unlocked desk drawer?"

"Sometimes. And sometimes they lock the drawers, but that doesn't make them all that much harder to open."

"You can pick locks?"

"A limited and eccentric talent," he allowed, "but it's all I know."

"How did you get in here? I suppose you picked the office lock."

"Hardly a great challenge."

"But how did you get past Eddie?"

"Eddie? Oh, you must be talking about the chap in the lobby. He's not quite as formidable as the Berlin Wall, you know. I got here around eight. They tend to be less suspicious at an earlier hour. I scrawled a name on the sheet and walked on by. Then I found an empty office that they'd already finished cleaning and curled up on the couch for a nap."

"You're kidding."

"Have I ever lied to you in the past? The cleaning crew leaves at midnight. At about that time I let myself out of Mr. Higginbotham's office—that's where I've taken to napping, he's a patent attorney with the most comfortable old leather couch. And then I make my rounds."

She looked at him. "You've come to this building before."

"I stop by every little once in a while."

"You make it sound like a vending machine route."

"There are similarities, aren't there? I never looked at it that way."

"And then you make your rounds. You break into offices—"

"I never break anything. Let's say I let myself into offices."

"And steal money from desks—"

"Also jewelry, when I run across it. Anything valuable and portable. Sometimes there's a safe. That saves a lot of looking around. You know right away that's where they keep the good stuff."

"And you can open safes?"

"Not every safe," he said modestly, "and not every single time, but—" he switched to a Cockney accent "—I has the touch, mum."

"And then what do you do? Wait until morning to leave?"

"What for? I'm well-dressed. I look respectable. Besides, security guards are posted to keep unauthorized persons out of a building, not to prevent them from leaving. It might be different if I tried rolling a Xerox machine through the lobby, but I don't steal anything that won't fit in my pockets or my attaché case. And I don't wear my rubber gloves when I saunter past the guard. That wouldn't do."

"I don't suppose it would. What do I call you?"

"'That damned burglar,' I suppose. That's what everybody else calls me. But you—" he extended a rubber-covered forefinger "—you may call me Bernie."

"Bernie the Burglar."

"And what shall I call you?"

"Elaine'll do."

"Elaine," he said. "Elaine, Elaine. Not Elaine Halder, by any chance?"

"How did you—?"

"Elaine Halder," he said. "And that explains what brings you to these offices in the middle of the night. You look startled. I can't imagine why. 'You know my methods, Watson.' What's the matter?"

"Nothing."

"Don't be frightened, for God's sake. Knowing your name doesn't give me mystical powers over your destiny. I just have a good memory and your name stuck in it." He crooked a thumb at a closed door on the far side of the room. "I've already been in the boss's office. I saw your note on his desk. I'm afraid I'll have to admit I read it. I'm a snoop. It's a serious character defect, I know."

"Like larceny."

"Something along those lines. Let's see now. Elaine Halder leaves the office, having placed on her boss's desk a letter of resignation. Elaine Halder returns in the small hours of the morning. A subtle pattern begins to emerge, my dear."

"Oh?"

"Of course. You've had second thoughts and you want to retrieve the letter before himself gets a chance to read it. Not a bad idea, given some of the choice things you had to say about him. Just let me open up for you, all right? I'm the tidy type and I locked up after I was through in there."

"Did you find anything to steal?"

"Eighty-five bucks and a pair of gold cuff links." He bent over the lock, probing its innards with a splinter of spring steel. "Nothing to write home about, but every little bit helps. I'm sure you have a key that fits this door— you had to in order to leave the resignation in the first place, didn't you? But how many chances do I get to show off? Not that a lock like this one presents much of a challenge, not to the nimble digits of Bernie the Burglar, and—ah, *there* we are!"

"Extraordinary."

"It's so seldom I have an audience."

He stood aside, held the door for her. On the threshold she was struck by the notion that there would be a dead body in the private office. George Tavistock himself, slumped over his desk with the figured hilt of a letter opener protruding from his back.

But of course there was no such thing. The office was devoid of clutter, let alone corpses, nor was there any sign that it had been lately burglarized.

A single sheet of paper lay on top of the desk blotter. She walked over, picked it up. Her eyes scanned its half dozen sentences as if she were reading them for the first time, then dropped to the elaborately styled signature, a far cry from the loose scrawl with which she'd signed the register in the lobby.

She read the note through again, then put it back where it had been.

"Not changing your mind again?"

She shook her head. "I never changed it in the first place. That's not why I came back here tonight."

"You couldn't have dropped in just for the pleasure of my company."

"I might have, if I'd known you were going to be here. No, I came back because—" She paused, drew a deliberate breath. "You might say I wanted to clean out my desk."

"Didn't you already do that? Isn't your desk right across there? The one with your name plate on it? Forward of me, I know, but I already had a peek, and the drawers bore a striking resemblance to the cupboard of one Ms. Hubbard."

"You went through my desk."

He spread his hands apologetically. "I meant nothing personal," he said. "At the time, I didn't even know you."

"That's a point."

"And searching an empty desk isn't that great an invasion of privacy, is it? Nothing to be seen beyond paper clips and rubber bands and the odd felt-tipped pen. So if you've come to clean out that lot—"

"I meant it metaphorically," she explained. "There are things in this office that belong to me. Projects I worked on that I ought to have copies of to show to prospective employers."

"And won't Mr. Tavistock see to it that you get copies?"

She laughed sharply. "You don't know the man," she said.

"And thank God for that. I couldn't rob someone I knew."

"He would think I intended to divulge corporate secrets to the competition. The minute he reads my letter of resignation I'll be persona non grata in this office. I probably won't even be able to get into the building.

I didn't even realize any of this until I'd gotten home tonight, and I didn't really know what to do, and then—"

"Then you decided to try a little burglary."

"Hardly that."

"Oh?"

"I have a key."

"And I have a cunning little piece of spring steel, and both perform the signal function of admitting us where we have no right to be."

"But I work here!"

"Worked."

"My resignation hasn't been accepted yet. I'm still an employee."

"Technically. Still, you've come like a thief in the night. You may have signed in downstairs and let yourself in with a key, and you're not wearing gloves or padding around in crepe-soled shoes, but we're not all that different, you and I, are we?"

She set her jaw. "I have a right to the fruits of my labor," she said.

"And so have I, and heaven help the person whose property rights get in our way."

She walked around him to the three-drawer filing cabinet to the right of the desk. It was locked.

She turned, but Bernie was already at her elbow. "Allow me," he said, and in no time at all he had tickled the locking mechanism and was drawing the top drawer open.

"Thank you," she said.

"Oh, don't thank me," he said. "Professional courtesy. No thanks required."

SHE WAS busy for the next thirty minutes, selecting documents from the filing cabinet and from Tavistock's desk, as well as a few items from the unlocked cabinets in the outer office. She ran everything through the Xerox copier and replaced the originals where she'd found them. While she was doing all this, her burglar friend worked his way through the office's remaining desks. He was in no evident hurry, and it struck her that he was deliberately dawdling so as not to finish before her.

Now and then she would look up from what she was doing to observe him at his work. Once she caught him looking at her, and when their eyes met he winked and smiled, and she felt her cheeks burning.

He was attractive, certainly. And likable, and in no way intimidating. Nor did he come across like a criminal. His speech was that of an educated person, he had an eye for clothes, his manners were impeccable—

What on earth was she thinking of?

BY THE time she had finished she had an inch-thick sheaf of paper in a manila file folder. She slipped her coat on, tucked the folder under her arm.

"You're certainly neat," he said. "A place for everything and everything right back in its place. I like that."

"Well, you're that way yourself, aren't you? You even take the trouble to lock up after yourself."

"It's not that much trouble. And there's a point to it. If one doesn't leave a mess, sometimes it takes them weeks to realize they've been robbed. The longer it takes, the less chance anybody'll figure out whodunit."

"And here I thought you were just naturally neat."

"As it happens I am, but it's a professional asset. Of course your neatness has much the same purpose, doesn't it? They'll never know you've been here tonight, especially since you haven't actually taken anything away with you. Just copies."

"That's right."

"Speaking of which, would you care to put them in my attaché case? So that you aren't noticed leaving the building with them in hand? I'll grant you the chap downstairs wouldn't notice an earthquake if it registered less than seven-point-four on the Richter scale, but it's that seemingly pointless attention to detail that enables me to persist in my chosen occupation instead of making license plates and sewing mail sacks as a guest of the governor. Are you ready, Elaine? Or would you like to take one last look around for auld lang syne?"

"I've had my last look around. And I'm not much on auld lang syne."

He held the door for her, switched off the overhead lights, drew the door shut. While she locked it with her key he stripped off his rubber gloves and put them in the case where her papers reposed. Then, side by side, they walked the length of the corridor to the elevator. Her footsteps echoed. His, cushioned by his crepe soles, were quite soundless.

Hers stopped, too, when they reached the elevator, and they waited in silence. They had met, she thought, as thieves in the night, and now were going to pass like ships in the night.

The elevator came, floated them down to the lobby. The lobby guard looked up at them, neither recognition nor interest showing in his eyes. She said, "Hi, Eddie. Everything going all right?"

"Hey, how ya doin'," he said.

There were only three entries below hers on the register sheet, three persons who'd arrived after her. She signed herself out, listing the time after a glance at her watch: She'd been upstairs for better than an hour and a half.

Outside, the wind had an edge to it. She turned to him, glanced at his attaché case, suddenly remembered the first schoolboy who'd carried her books. She could surely have carried her own books, just as she could have safely carried the folder of papers past Eagle-eye Eddie.

Still, it was not unpleasant to have one's books carried.

"Well," she began, "I'd better take my papers, and—"

"Where are you headed?"

"Seventy-sixth Street."

"East or west?"

"East. But—"

"We'll share a cab," he said. "Compliments of petty cash." And he was at the curb, a hand raised, and a cab appeared as if conjured up, and then he was holding the door for her.

She got in.

"Seventy-sixth," he told the driver. "And what?

"Lexington," she said.

"Lexington," he said.

Her mind raced during the taxi ride. It was all over the place and she couldn't keep up with it. She felt in turn like a schoolgirl, like a damsel in peril, like Grace Kelly in a Hitchcock film. When the cab reached her corner she indicated her building, and he leaned forward to relay the information to the driver.

"Would you like to come up for coffee?"

The line had run through her mind like a mantra in the course of the ride. Yet she couldn't believe she was actually speaking the words.

"Yes," he said. "I'd like that."

SHE STEELED herself as they approached her doorman, but the man was discretion personified. He didn't even greet her by name, merely holding the door for her and her escort and wishing them a good night. Upstairs, she thought of demanding that Bernie open her door without the keys, but decided she didn't want any demonstrations just then of her essential vulnerability. She unlocked the several locks herself.

"I'll make coffee," she said. "Or would you just as soon have a drink?"

"Sounds good."

"Scotch? Or cognac?"

"Cognac."

While she was pouring the drinks he walked around her living room, looking at the pictures on the walls and the books on the shelves. Guests did this sort of thing all the time, but this particular guest was a criminal, after all, and so she imagined him taking a burglar's inventory of her possessions. That Chagall aquatint he was studying—she'd paid five hundred for it at auction and it was probably worth close to three times that by now.

Surely he'd have better luck foraging in her apartment than in a suite of deserted offices.

Surely he'd realize as much himself.

She handed him his brandy. "To criminal enterprise," he said, and she raised her glass in response.

"I'll give you those papers. Before I forget."

"All right."

He opened the attaché case, handed them over. She placed the folder on the coffee table and carried her brandy across to the window. The deep carpet muffled her footsteps as effectively as if she'd been the one wearing crepe-soled shoes.

You have nothing to be afraid of, she told herself. *And you're not afraid, and—*

"An impressive view," he said, close behind her.

"Yes."

"You could see your office from here. If that building weren't in the way."

"I was thinking that earlier."

"Beautiful," he said, softly, and then his arms were encircling her from behind and his lips were on the nape of her neck.

"'Elaine the fair, Elaine the lovable,'" he quoted. "'Elaine the lily maid of Astolat.'" His lips nuzzled her ear. "But you must hear that all the time."

She smiled. "Oh, not so often," she said. "Less often than you'd think."

THE SKY was just growing light when he left. She lay alone for a few minutes, then went to lock up after him. And laughed aloud when she found that he'd locked up after himself, without a key.

It was late but she didn't think she'd ever been less tired. She put up a fresh pot of coffee, poured a cup when it was ready, and sat at the kitchen table reading through the papers she'd taken from the office. She wouldn't have had half of them without Bernie's assistance, she realized. She could never have opened the file cabinet in Tavistock's office.

"Elaine the fair, Elaine the lovable. Elaine, the lily maid of Astolat."

She smiled.

A few minutes after nine, when she was sure Jennings Colliard would be at his desk, she dialed his private number.

"It's Andrea," she told him. "I succeeded beyond our wildest dreams. I've got copies of Tavistock's complete marketing plan for fall and winter, along with a couple of dozen test and survey reports and a lot of other documents you'll want a chance to analyze. And I put all the originals back where they came from, so nobody at Tavistock'll ever know what happened."

"Remarkable."

"I thought you'd approve. Having a key to their office helped, and knowing the doorman's name didn't hurt any. Oh, and I also have some news that's worth knowing. I don't know if George Tavistock is in his office yet, but if so he's reading a letter of resignation even as we speak. The Lily Maid of Astolat has had it."

"What are you talking about, Andrea?"

"Elaine Halder. She cleaned out her desk and left him a note saying bye-bye. I thought you'd like to be the first kid on your block to know that."

"And of course you're right."

"I'd come in now but I'm exhausted. Do you want to send a messenger over?"

"Right away. And you get some sleep."

"I intend to."

"You've done spectacularly well, Andrea. There will be something extra in your stocking."

"I thought there might be," she said.

She hung up the phone and stood once again at the window, looking out at the city, reviewing the night's events. It had been quite perfect, she decided, and if there was the slightest flaw it was that she'd missed the Cary Grant movie.

But it would be on again soon. They ran it frequently. People evidently liked that sort of thing.

THE BURGLAR
WHO DROPPED
IN ON ELVIS

"**I KNOW WHO YOU** are," she said. "Your name is Bernie Rhodenbarr. You're a burglar."

I glanced around, glad that the store was empty save for the two of us. It often is, but I'm not usually glad about it.

"Was," I said.

"Was?"

"Was. Past tense. I had a criminal past, and while I'd as soon keep it a secret I can't deny it. But I'm an antiquarian bookseller now, Miss Uh—"

"Danahy," she supplied. "Holly Danahy."

"Miss Danahy. A dealer in the wisdom of the ages. The errors of my youth are to be regretted, even deplored, but they're over and done with."

She gazed thoughtfully at me. She was a lovely creature, slender, pert, bright of eye and inquisitive of nose, and she wore a tailored suit and flowing bow tie that made her look at once yieldingly feminine and as coolly competent as a Luger.

"I think you're lying," she said. "I certainly hope so. Because an antiquarian bookseller is no good at all to me. What I need is a burglar."

"I wish I could help you."

"You can." She laid a cool-fingered hand on mine. "It's almost closing time. Why don't you lock up? I'll buy you a drink and tell you how you can qualify for an all-expenses-paid trip to Memphis. And possibly a whole lot more."

"You're not trying to sell me a time-share in a thriving resort community, are you?"

"Not hardly."

"Then what have I got to lose? The thing is, I usually have a drink after work with—"

"Carolyn Kaiser," she cut in. "Your best friend, she washes dogs two doors down the street at the Poodle Factory. You can call her and cancel."

My turn to gaze thoughtfully. "You seem to know a lot about me," I said.

"Sweetie," she said, "that's my job."

"I'M A reporter," she said. "For the *Weekly Galaxy*. If you don't know the paper, you must never get to the supermarket."

"I know it," I said. "But I have to admit I'm not what you'd call one of your regular readers."

"Well, I should hope not, Bernie. Our readers move their lips when they think. Our readers write letters in crayon because they're not allowed to have anything sharp. Our readers make the *Enquirer*'s readers look like Rhodes scholars. Our readers, face it, are D-U-M."

"Then why would they want to know about me?"

"They wouldn't, unless an extraterrestrial made you pregnant. That happen to you?"

"No, but Bigfoot ate my car."

She shook her head. "We already did that story. Last August, I think it was. The car was an AMC Gremlin with a hundred and ninety-two thousand miles on it."

"I suppose its time had come."

"That's what the owner said. He's got a new BMW now, thanks to the *Galaxy*. He can't spell it, but he can drive it like crazy."

I looked at her over the brim of my glass. "If you don't want to write about me," I said, "what do you need me for?"

"Ah, Bernie," she said. "Bernie the burglar. Sweetie pie, you're my ticket to Elvis."

"THE BEST possible picture," I told Carolyn, "would be a shot of Elvis in his coffin. The *Galaxy* loves shots like that, but in this case it would be counterproductive in the long run, because it might kill their big story, the one run they month after month."

"Which is that he's still alive."

"Right. Now the second-best possible picture, and better for their purposes overall, would be a shot of him alive, singing 'Love Me Tender' to a visitor from another planet. They get a chance at that picture every couple of days, and it's always some Elvis impersonator. Do you know how many full-time professional Elvis Presley impersonators there are in America today?"

"No."

"Neither do I, but I have a feeling Holly Danahy could probably supply a figure, and that it would be an impressive one. Anyway, the third-best possible picture, and the one she seems to want almost more than life itself, is a shot of the King's bedroom."

"At Graceland?"

"That's the one. Six thousand people visit Graceland every day. Two million of them walked through it last year."

"And none of them brought a camera?"

"Don't ask me how many cameras they brought, or how many rolls of film they shot. Or how many souvenir ashtrays and paintings on black velvet they bought and took home with them. But how many of them got above the first floor?"

"How many?"

"None. Nobody gets to go upstairs at Graceland. The staff isn't allowed up there, and people who've worked there for years have never set foot above the ground floor. And you can't bribe your way up there, either, according to Holly, and she knows because she tried, and she had all the

Galaxy's resources to play with. Two million people a year go to Graceland, and they'd all love to know what it looks like upstairs, and the *Weekly Galaxy* would just love to show them."

"Enter a burglar."

"That's it. That's Holly's masterstroke, the one designed to win her a bonus and a promotion. Enter an expert at illegal entry, a burglar. *Le burglar, c'est moi.* Name your price, she told me."

"And what did you tell her?"

"Twenty-five thousand dollars. You know why? All I could think of was that it sounded like a job for Nick Velvet. You remember him, the thief in the Ed Hoch stories who'll only steal worthless objects." I sighed. "When I think of all the worthless objects I've stolen over the years, and never once has anyone offered to pay me a fee of twenty-five grand for my troubles. Anyway, that was the price that popped into my head, so I tried it out on her. And she didn't even try to haggle."

"I think Nick Velvet raised his rates," Carolyn said. "I think his price went up in the last story or two."

I shook my head. "You see what happens? You fall behind on your reading and it costs you money."

HOLLY AND I flew first class from JFK to Memphis. The meal was still airline food, but the seats were so comfortable and the stewardess so attentive that I kept forgetting this.

"At the *Weekly Galaxy*," Holly said, sipping an after-dinner something-or-other, "everything's first class. Except the paper itself, of course."

We got our luggage, and a hotel courtesy car whisked us to the Howard Johnson's on Elvis Presley Boulevard, where we had adjoining rooms reserved. I was just about unpacked when Holly knocked on the door separating the two rooms. I unlocked it for her and she came in carrying a bottle of scotch and a full ice bucket.

"I wanted to stay at the Peabody," she said. "That's the great old downtown hotel and it's supposed to be wonderful, but here we're only a couple of blocks from Graceland, and I thought it would be more convenient."

"Makes sense," I agreed.

"But I wanted to see the ducks," she said. She explained that ducks were the symbol of the Peabody, or the mascots, or something. Every day the hotel's guests could watch the hotel's ducks waddle across the red carpet to the fountain in the middle of the lobby.

"Tell me something," she said. "How does a guy like you get into a business like this?"

"Bookselling?"

"Get real, honey. How'd you get to be a burglar? Not for the edification of our readers, because they couldn't care less. But to satisfy my own curiosity."

I sipped a drink while I told her the story of my misspent life, or as much of it as I felt like telling. She heard me out and put away four stiff scotches in the process, but if they had any effect on her I couldn't see it.

"And how about you?" I said after a while. "How did a nice girl like you—"

"Oh, Gawd," she said. "We'll save that for another evening, okay?" And then she was in my arms, smelling and feeling better than a body had a right to, and just as quickly she was out of them again and on her way to the door.

"You don't have to go," I said.

"Ah, but I do, Bernie. We've got a big day tomorrow. We're going to see Elvis, remember?"

She took the scotch with her. I poured out what remained of my own drink, finished unpacking, took a shower. I got into bed, and after fifteen or twenty minutes I got up and tried the door between our two rooms, but she had locked it on her side. I went back to bed.

OUR TOUR guide's name was Stacy. She wore the standard Graceland uniform, a blue-and-white-striped shirt over navy chinos, and she looked like someone who'd been unable to decide whether to become a stewardess or a cheerleader. Cleverly, she'd chosen a job that combined both professions.

"There were generally a dozen guests crowded around this dining table," she told us. "Dinner was served nightly between nine and ten PM, and Elvis always sat right there at the head of the table. Not because he

59

was head of the family but because it gave him the best view of the big color TV. Now that's one of fourteen sets here at Graceland, so you know how much Elvis liked to watch TV."

"Was that the regular china?" someone wanted to know.

"Yes, ma'am, and the name of the pattern is Buckingham. Isn't it pretty?"

I could run down the whole tour for you, but what's the point? Either you've been there yourself or you're planning to go or you don't care, and at the rate people are signing up for the tours, I don't think there are many of you in the last group. Elvis was a good pool player, and his favorite game was rotation. Elvis ate his breakfast in the Jungle Room, off a cypress coffee table. Elvis's own favorite singer was Dean Martin. Elvis liked peacocks, and at one time over a dozen of them roamed the grounds of Graceland. Then they started eating the paint off the cars, which Elvis liked even more than he liked peacocks, so he donated them to the Memphis Zoo. The peacocks, not the cars.

There was a gold rope across the mirrored staircase, and what looked like an electric eye a couple of stairs up. "We don't allow tourists into the upstairs," our guide chirped. "Remember, Graceland is a private home and Elvis's aunt Miss Delta Biggs still lives here. Now I can tell you what's upstairs. Elvis's bedroom is located directly above the living room and music room. His office is also upstairs, and there's Lisa Marie's bedroom, and dressing rooms and bathrooms as well."

"And does his aunt live up there?" someone asked.

"No, sir. She lives downstairs, through that door over to your left. None of us have ever been upstairs. Nobody goes there anymore."

"I BET he's up there now," Holly said. "In a La-Z-Boy with his feet up, eating one of his famous peanut butter and banana sandwiches and watching three television sets at once."

"And listening to Dean Martin," I said. "What do you really think?"

"What do I really think? I think he's down in Paraguay playing three-handed pinochle with James Dean and Adolf Hitler. Did you know that

Hitler master-minded Argentina's invasion of the Falkland Islands? We ran that story but it didn't do as well as we hoped."

"Your readers didn't remember Hitler?"

"Hitler was no problem for them. But they didn't know what the Falklands were. Seriously, where do I think Elvis is? I think he's in the grave we just looked at, surrounded by his nearest and dearest. Unfortunately, 'Elvis Still Dead' is not a headline that sells papers."

"I guess not."

We were back in my room at the HoJo, eating a lunch Holly had ordered from room service. It reminded me of our in-flight meal the day before, luxurious but not terribly good.

"Well," she said brightly, "have you figured out how we're going to get in?"

"You saw the place," I said. "They've got gates and guards and alarm systems everywhere. I don't know what's upstairs, but it's a more closely guarded secret than Zsa Zsa Gabor's true age."

"That'd be easy to find," Holly said. "We could just hire somebody to marry her."

"Graceland is impregnable," I went on, hoping we could drop the analogy right there. "It's almost as bad as Fort Knox."

Her face fell. "I was sure you could find a way in."

"Maybe I can."

"But—"

"For one. Not for two. It'd be too risky for you, and you don't have the skills for it. Could you shinny down a gutterspout?"

"If I had to."

"Well, you won't have to, because you won't be going in." I paused for thought. "You'd have a lot of work to do," I said. "On the outside, coordinating things."

"I can handle it."

"And there would be expenses, plenty of them."

"No problem."

"I'd need a camera that can take pictures in full dark. I can't risk a flash."

"That's easy. We can handle that."

"I'll need to rent a helicopter, and I'll have to pay the pilot enough to guarantee his silence."

"A cinch."

"I'll need a diversion. Something fairly dramatic."

"I can create a diversion. With all the resources of the *Galaxy* at my disposal, I could divert a river."

"That shouldn't be necessary. But all of this is going to cost money."

"Money," she said, "is no object."

"SO YOU'RE a friend of Carolyn's," Lucian Leeds said. "She's wonderful, isn't she? You know, she and I are the next closest thing to blood kin."

"Oh?"

"A former lover of hers and a former lover of mine were brother and sister. Well, sister and brother, actually. So that makes Carolyn my something-in-law, doesn't it?"

"I guess it must."

"Of course," he said, "by the same token, I must be related to half the known world. Still, I'm real fond of our Carolyn. If I can help you—"

I told him what I needed. Lucian Leeds was an interior decorator and a dealer in art and antiques. "Of course I've been to Graceland," he said. "Probably a dozen times, because whenever a friend or relative visits that's where one has to take them. It's an experience that somehow never palls."

"I don't suppose you've ever been on the second floor."

"No, nor have I been presented at court. Of the two, I suppose I'd prefer the second floor at Graceland. One can't help wondering, can one?" He closed his eyes, concentrating. "My imagination is beginning to work," he announced.

"Give it free rein."

"I know just the house, too. It's off Route 51 across the Mississippi state line, just this side of Hernando. Oh, and I know someone with an Egyptian piece that would be perfect. How soon would everything have to be ready?"

"Tomorrow night?"

"Impossible. The day after tomorrow is barely possible. Just barely. I really ought to have a week to do it right."

"Well, do it as right as you can."

"I'll need trucks and schleppers, of course. I'll have rental charges to pay, needless to say, and I'll have to give something to the old girl who owns the house. First I'll need to sweet-talk her, but there'll have to be something tangible in it for her as well, I'm afraid. But all of this is going to cost you money."

That had a familiar ring to it. I almost got caught up in the rhythm of it and told him money was no object, but I managed to restrain myself. If money wasn't the object, what was I doing in Memphis?

HERE'S THE camera," Holly said. "It's all loaded with infrared film. No flash, and you can take pictures with it at the bottom of a coal mine."

"That's good," I said, "because that's probably where I'll wind up if they catch me. We'll do it the day after tomorrow. Today's what, Wednesday? I'll go in Friday."

"I should be able to give you a terrific diversion."

"I hope so," I said. "I'll probably need it."

THURSDAY MORNING I found my helicopter pilot. "Yeah, I could do it," he said. "Cost you two hundred dollars, though."

"I'll give you five hundred."

He shook his head. "One thing I never do," he said, "is get to haggling over prices. I said two hundred, and—wait a darn minute."

"Take all the time you need."

"You weren't haggling me down," he said. 'You were haggling me up. I never heard tell of such a thing."

"I'm willing to pay extra," I said, "so that you'll tell people the right story afterward. If anybody asks."

"What do you want me to tell 'em?"

"That somebody you never met before in your life paid you to fly over Graceland, hover over the mansion, lower your rope ladder, raise the ladder, and then fly away."

He thought about this for a full minute. "But that's what you said you wanted me to do," he said.

"I know."

"So you're fixing to pay me an extra three hundred dollars just to tell people the truth."

"If anybody should ask."

"You figure they will?"

"They might," I said. "It would be best if you said it in such a way that they thought you were lying."

"Nothing to it," he said. "Nobody ever believes a word I say. I'm a pretty honest guy, but I guess I don't look it."

"You don't," I said. "That's why I picked you."

THAT NIGHT Holly and I dressed up and took a cab downtown to the Peabody. The restaurant there was named Dux, and they had *canard aux cerises* on the menu, but it seemed curiously sacrilegious to have it there. We both ordered the blackened redfish. She had two dry Rob Roys first, most of the dinner wine, and a Stinger afterward. I had a Bloody Mary for openers, and my after-dinner drink was a cup of coffee. I felt like a cheap date.

Afterward we went back to my room and she worked on the scotch while we discussed strategy. From time to time she would put her drink down and kiss me, but as soon as things threatened to get interesting she'd draw away and cross her legs and pick up her pencil and reach for her drink.

"You're a tease," I said.

"I am not," she insisted. "But I want to, you know, save it."

"For the wedding?"

"For the celebration. After we get the pictures, after we carry the day. You'll be the conquering hero and I'll throw roses at your feet."

"Roses?"

"And myself. I figured we could take a suite at the Peabody and never leave the room except to see the ducks. You know, we never did watch the ducks do their famous walk. Can't you just picture them waddling across the red carpet and quacking their heads off?"

"Can't you just picture what they go through cleaning that carpet?"

She pretended not to have heard me. "I'm glad we didn't have duckling," she said. "It would have seemed cannibalistic." She fixed her eyes on me. She'd had enough booze to induce coma in a six-hundred-pound gorilla, but her eyes looked as clear as ever. "Actually," she said, "I'm very strongly attracted to you, Bernie. But I want to wait. You can understand that, can't you?"

"I could," I said gravely, "if I knew I was coming back."

"What do you mean?"

"It would be great to be the conquering hero," I said, "and find you and the roses at my feet, but suppose I come home on my shield instead? I could get killed out there."

"Are you serious?"

"Think of me as a kid who enlisted the day after Pearl Harbor, Holly. And you're his girlfriend, asking him to wait until the war's over. Holly, what if that kid doesn't come home? What if he leaves his bones bleaching on some little hellhole in the South Pacific?"

"Oh my God," she said. "I never thought of that." She put down her pencil and notebook. "You're right, dammit. I *am* a tease. I'm worse than that." She uncrossed her legs. "I'm thoughtless and heartless. Oh, Bernie!"

"There, there," I said.

GRACELAND CLOSES every evening at six. At precisely five-thirty Friday afternoon, a girl named Moira Beth Calloway detached herself from her tour group. "I'm coming, Elvis!" she cried, and she lowered her head and ran full speed for the staircase. She was over the gold rope and on the sixth step before the first guard laid a hand on her.

Bells rang, sirens squealed, and all hell broke loose. "Elvis is calling me," Moira Beth insisted, her eyes rolling wildly. "He needs me, he wants me, he loves me tender. Get your hands off me. Elvis! I'm coming, Elvis!"

I.D. in Moira Beth's purse supplied her name and indicated that she was seventeen years old, and a student at Mount St. Joseph Academy in Millington, Tennessee. This was not strictly true, in that she was actually twenty-two years old, a member of Actors Equity, and a resident of Brooklyn Heights. Her name was not Moira Beth Calloway, either. It was (and still is) Rona Jellicoe. I think it may have been something else in the dim dark past before it became Rona Jellicoe, but who cares?

While a variety of people, many of them wearing navy chinos and blue-and-white-striped shirts, did what they could to calm down Moira Beth, a middle-aged couple in the Pool Room went into their act. "Air!" the man cried, clutching at his throat. "Air! I can't breathe!" And he fell down, flailing at the wall, where Stacy had told us some 750 yards of pleated fabric had been installed.

"Help him," cried his wife. "He can't breathe! He's dying! He needs air!" And she ran to the nearest window and heaved it open, setting off whatever alarms hadn't already been shrieking over Moira Beth's assault on the staircase.

Meanwhile, in the TV room, done in the exact shades of yellow and blue used in Cub Scout uniforms, a gray squirrel had raced across the rug and was now perched on top of the jukebox. "Look at that awful squirrel!" a woman was screaming. "Somebody get that squirrel! He's gonna kill us all!"

Her fear would have been harder to credit if people had known that the poor rodent had entered Graceland in her handbag, and that she'd been able to release it without being seen because of the commotion in the other room. Her fear was contagious, though, and the people who caught it weren't putting on an act.

In the Jungle Room, where Elvis's *Moody Blue* album had actually been recorded, a woman fainted. She'd been hired to do just that, but other unpaid fainters were dropping like flies all over the mansion. And, while all of this activity was hitting its absolute peak, a helicopter made its noisy way through the sky over Graceland, hovering for several long minutes over the roof.

The security staff at Graceland couldn't have been better. Almost immediately two men emerged from a shed carrying an extension ladder, and in no time at all they had it propped against the side of the building. One of them held it while the other scrambled up it to the roof.

By the time he got there, the helicopter was going *pocketa-pocketa-pocketa*, and disappearing off to the west. The security man raced around the roof but didn't see anyone. Within the next ten minutes, two others joined him on the roof and searched it thoroughly. They found a tennis sneaker, but that was all they found.

AT A quarter to five the next morning I let myself into my room at the Howard Johnson's and knocked on the door to Holly's room. There was no response. I knocked again, louder, then gave up and used the phone. I could hear it ringing in her room, but evidently she couldn't.

So I used the skills God gave me and opened her door. She was sprawled out on the bed, with her clothes scattered where she had flung them. The trail of clothing began at the scotch bottle on top of the television set. The set was on, and some guy with a sport jacket and an Ipana smile was explaining how you could get cash advances on your credit cards and buy penny stocks, an enterprise that struck me as a lot riskier than burglarizing mansions by helicopter.

Holly didn't want to wake up, but when I got past the veil of sleep she came to as if transistorized. One moment she was comatose and the next she was sitting up, eyes bright, an expectant look on her face. "Well?" she demanded.

"I shot the whole roll."

"You got in."

"Uh-huh."

"And you got out."

"Right again."

"And you got the pictures." She clapped her hands, giddy with glee. "I knew it," she said. "I was a positive genius to think of you. Oh, they ought to give me a bonus, a raise, a promotion, oh, I bet I get a company Cadillac next year instead of a lousy Chevy, oh, I'm on a roll, Bernie, I swear I'm on a roll!"

"That's great."

"You're limping," she said. "Why are you limping? Because you've only got one shoe on, that's why. What happened to your other shoe?"

"I lost it on the roof."

"God," she said. She got off the bed and began picking up her clothes from the floor and putting them on, following the trail back to the scotch bottle, which evidently had one drink left in it. "Ahhhh," she said, putting it down empty. "You know, when I saw them race up the ladder I thought you were finished. How did you get away from them?"

"It wasn't easy."

"I bet. And you managed to get down onto the second floor? And into his bedroom? What's it like?"

"I don't know."

"You don't know? Weren't you in there?"

"Not until it was pitch-dark. I hid in a hall closet and locked myself in. They gave the place a pretty thorough search but nobody had a key to the closet. I don't think there is one, I locked it by picking it. I let myself out somewhere around two in the morning and found my way into the bedroom. There was enough light to keep from bumping into things but not enough to tell what it was I wasn't bumping into. I just walked around pointing the camera and shooting."

She wanted more details, but I don't think she paid very much attention to them. I was in the middle of a sentence when she picked up the phone and made a plane reservation to Miami.

"They've got me on a ten-twenty flight," she said. "I'll get these right into the office and we'll get a check out to you as soon as they're developed. What's the matter?"

"I don't think I want a check," I said. "And I don't want to give you the film without getting paid."

"Oh, come on," she said. "You can trust us, for God's sake."

"Why don't you trust me instead?"

"You mean pay you without seeing what we're paying for? Bernie, you're a burglar. How can I trust you?"

"You're the *Weekly Galaxy*," I said. "*Nobody* can trust you."

"You've got a point," she said.

"We'll get the film developed here," I said. "I'm sure there are some good commercial photo labs in Memphis and that they can handle infrared film. First you'll call your office and have them wire cash here or set up an interbank transfer, and as soon as you see what's on the film you can hand over the money. You can even fax them one of the prints first to get approval, if you think that'll make a difference."

"Oh, they'll love that," she said. "My boss loves it when I fax him stuff."

"AND THAT'S what happened," I told Carolyn. "The pictures came out really beautifully. I don't know how Lucian Leeds turned up all those Egyptian pieces, but they looked great next to the 1940s Wurlitzer jukebox and the seven-foot statue of Mickey Mouse. I thought Holly was going to die of happiness when she realized the thing next to Mickey was a sarcophagus. She couldn't decide which tack to take—that he's mummified and they're keeping him in it or he's alive and really weird and uses it for a bed."

"Maybe they can have a reader poll. Call a nine hundred number and vote."

"You wouldn't believe how loud helicopters are when you're inside them. I just dropped the ladder and pulled it back in again. And tossed an extra sneaker on the roof."

"And wore its mate when you saw Holly."

"Yeah, I thought a little verisimilitude wouldn't hurt. The chopper pilot dropped me back at the hangar and I caught a ride down to the house in Mississippi. I walked around the room Lucian had decorated for the occasion, admired everything, then turned out all the lights and took my pictures. They'll be running the best ones in the *Galaxy*."

"And you got paid."

"Twenty-five grand, and everybody's happy, and I didn't cheat anybody or steal anything. The *Galaxy* got some great pictures that'll sell a lot of copies of their horrible paper. The readers get a peek at a room no has ever seen before."

"And the folks at Graceland?"

"They get a good security drill," I said. "Holly created a peach of a diversion to hide my entering the building. What it hid, of course, was my *not* entering the building, and that fact should stay hidden forever. Most of the Graceland people have never seen Elvis's bedroom, so they'll think the photos are legit. The few who know better will just figure my pictures didn't come out, or that they weren't exciting enough, so the *Galaxy* decided to run fakes instead. Everybody with any sense figures the paper's a fake anyway, so what difference does it make?"

"Was Holly a fake?"

"Not really. I'd say she's an authentic specimen of what she is. Of course her little fantasy about a hot weekend watching the ducks blew away with the morning mist. All she wanted to do was get back to Florida and collect her bonus."

"So it's just as well you got your bonus ahead of time. You'll hear from her again the next time the *Galaxy* needs a burglar."

"Well, I'd do it again," I said. "My mother was always hoping I'd go into journalism. I wouldn't have waited so long if I'd known it would be so much fun."

"Yeah," she said.

"What's the matter?"

"Nothing, Bern."

"Come on. What is it?"

"Oh, I don't know. I just you wish, you know, that you'd gone in there and got the real pictures. He could be in there, Bern. I mean, why else would they make such a big thing out of keeping people out of there? Did you ever stop to ask yourself that?"

"Carolyn—"

"I know," she said. "You think I'm nuts. But there are a lot of people like me, Bern."

"It's a good thing," I told her. "Where would the *Galaxy* be without you?"

THE BURGLAR WHO SMELLED SMOKE

BY LYNNE WOOD BLOCK AND LAWRENCE BLOCK

I WAS GEARING UP to poke the bell a second time when the door opened. I'd been expecting Karl Bellermann, and instead I found myself facing a woman with soft blond hair framing an otherwise severe, high-cheekboned face. She looked as if she'd been repeatedly disappointed in life but was damned if she would let it get to her.

I gave my name and she nodded in recognition. "Yes, Mr. Rhodenbarr," she said. "Karl is expecting you. I can't disturb him now as he's in the library with his books. If you'll come into the sitting room I'll bring you some coffee, and Karl will be with you in—" she consulted her watch "—in just twelve minutes."

In twelve minutes it would be noon, which was when Karl had told me to arrive. I'd taken a train from New York and a cab from the train station, and good connections had got me there twelve minutes early, and evidently I could damn well cool my heels for all twelve of those minutes.

I was faintly miffed, but I wasn't much surprised. Karl Bellermann, arguably the country's leading collector of crime fiction, had taken a cue from one of the genre's greatest creations, Rex Stout's incomparable Nero Wolfe. Wolfe, an orchid fancier, spent an inviolate two hours in the morning and two hours in the afternoon with his plants, and would brook no disturbance at such times. Bellermann, no more flexible in real life than Wolfe was in fiction, scheduled even longer sessions with his books, and would neither greet visitors nor take phone calls while communing with them.

The sitting room where the blond woman led me was nicely appointed, and the chair where she planted me was comfortable enough. The coffee she poured was superb, rich and dark and winy. I picked up the latest issue of *Ellery Queen* and was halfway through a new Peter Lovesey story and just finishing my second cup of coffee when the door opened and Karl Bellermann strode in.

"Bernie," he said. "Bernie Rhodenbarr."

"Karl."

"So good of you to come. You had no trouble finding us?"

"I took a taxi from the train station. The driver knew the house."

He laughed. "I'll bet he did. And I'll bet I know what he called it. 'Bellermann's Folly,' yes?"

"Well," I said.

"Please, don't spare my feelings. That's what all the local rustics call it. They hold in contempt that which they fail to understand. To their eyes, the architecture is overly ornate, and too much a mixture of styles, at once a Rhenish castle and an alpine chalet. And the library dwarfs the rest of the house, like the tail that wags the dog. Your driver is very likely a man who owns a single book, the Bible given to him for Confirmation and unopened ever since. That a man might choose to devote to his books the greater portion of his house—and, indeed, the greater portion of his life— could not fail to strike him as an instance of remarkable eccentricity." His eyes twinkled. "Although he might phrase it differently."

Indeed he had. "The guy's a nut case," the driver had reported confidently. "One look at his house and you'll see for yourself. He's only eating with one chopstick."

A FEW minutes later I sat down to lunch with Karl Bellermann, and there were no chopsticks in evidence. He ate with a fork, and he was every bit as agile with it as the fictional orchid fancier. Our meal consisted of a crown loin of pork with roasted potatoes and braised cauliflower, and Bellermann put away a second helping of everything.

I don't know where he put it. He was a long lean gentleman in his mid-fifties, with a full head of iron-gray hair and a mustache a little darker than the hair on his head. He'd dressed rather elaborately for a day at home with his books—a tie, a vest, a Donegal tweed jacket—and I didn't flatter myself that it was on my account. I had a feeling he chose a similar get-up seven days a week, and I wouldn't have been surprised to learn he put on a black tie every night for dinner.

He carried most of the lunchtime conversation, talking about books he'd read, arguing the relative merits of Hammett and Chandler, musing on the likelihood that female private eyes in fiction had come to out-number their real-life counterparts. I didn't feel called upon to contribute much, and Mrs. Bellermann never uttered a word except to offer dessert (apfelküchen, lighter than air and sweeter than revenge) and coffee (the mixture as before but a fresh pot of it, and seemingly richer and darker and stronger and winier this time around). Karl and I both turned down a second piece of the cake and said yes to a second cup of coffee, and then Karl turned significantly to his wife and gave her a formal nod.

"Thank you, Eva," he said. And she rose, all but curtseyed, and left the room.

"She leaves us to our brandy and cigars," he said, "but it's too early in the day for spirits, and no one smokes in Schloss Bellermann."

"Schloss Bellermann?"

"A joke of mine. If the world calls it Bellermann's Folly, why shouldn't Bellermann call it his castle? Eh?"

"Why not?"

He looked at his watch. "But let me show you my library," he said, "and then you can show me what you've brought me."

DIAGONAL MULLIONS divided the library door into a few dozen diamond-shaped sections, each set with a mirrored pane of glass. The effect was unusual, and I asked if they were one-way mirrors.

"Like the ones in police stations?" He raised an eyebrow. "Your past is showing, eh, Bernie? But no, it is even more of a trick than the police play on criminals. On the other side of the mirror—" he clicked a fingernail against a pane "—is solid steel an inch and a half thick. The library walls themselves are reinforced with steel sheeting. The exterior walls are concrete, reinforced with steel rods. And look at this lock."

It was a Poulard, its mechanism intricate beyond description, its key one that not a locksmith in ten thousand could duplicate.

"Pickproof," he said. "They guarantee it."

"So I understand."

He slipped the irreproducible key into the impregnable lock and opened the unbreachable door. Inside was a room two full stories tall, with a system of ladders leading to the upper levels. The library, as tall as the house itself, had an eighteen-foot ceiling paneled in light and dark wood in a sunburst pattern. Wall-to-wall carpet covered the floor, and oriental rugs in turn covered most of the broadloom. The walls, predictably enough, were given over to floor-to-ceiling bookshelves, with the shelves themselves devoted entirely to books. There were no paintings, no Chinese ginger jars, no bronze animals, no sets of armor, no cigar humidors, no framed photographs of family members, no hand-colored engravings of Victoria Falls, no hunting trophies, no Lalique figurines, no Limoges boxes. Nothing but books, sometimes embraced by bronze bookends, but mostly extending without interruption from one end of a section of shelving to the other.

"Books," he said reverently—and, I thought, unnecessarily. I own a bookstore, I can recognize books when I see them.

"Books," I affirmed.

"I believe they are happy."

"Happy?"

"You are surprised? Why should objects lack feelings, especially objects of such a sensitive nature as books? And, if a book can have feelings, these books ought to be happy. They are owned and tended by a man who cares deeply for them. And they are housed in a room perfectly designed for their safety and comfort."

"It certainly looks that way."

He nodded. "Two windows only, on the north wall, of course, so that no direct sunlight ever enters the room. Sunlight fades book spines, bleaches the ink of a dust jacket. It is a book's enemy, and it cannot gain entry here."

"That's good," I said. "My store faces south, and the building across the street blocks some of the sunlight, but a little gets through. I have to make sure I don't keep any of the better volumes where the light can get at them."

"You should paint the windows black," he said, "or hang thick curtains. Or both."

"Well, I like to keep an eye on the street," I said. "And my cat likes to sleep in the sunlit window."

He made a face. "A cat? In a room full of books?"

"He'd be safe," I said, "even in a room full of rocking chairs. He's a Manx. And he's an honest working cat. I used to have mice damaging the books, and that stopped the day he moved in."

"No mice can get in here," Bellermann said, "and neither can cats, with their hair and their odor. Mold cannot attack my books, or mildew. You feel the air?"

"The air?"

"A constant sixty-four degrees Fahrenheit," he said. "On the cool side, but perfect for my books. I put on a jacket and I am perfectly comfortable. And, as you can see, most of them are already wearing their jackets. Dust jackets! Ha ha!"

"Ha ha," I agreed.

"The humidity is sixty per cent," he went on. "It never varies. Too dry and the glue dries out. Too damp and the pages rot. Neither can happen here."

"That's reassuring."

"I would say so. The air is filtered regularly, with not only air conditioning but special filters to remove pollutants that are truly microscopic. No book could ask for a safer or more comfortable environment."

I sniffed the air. It was cool, and neither too moist nor too dry, and as immaculate as modern science could make it. My nose wrinkled, and I picked up a whiff of something.

"What about fire?" I wondered.

"Steel walls, steel doors, triple-glazed windows with heat resistant bulletproof glass. Special insulation in the walls and ceiling and floor. The whole house could burn to the ground, Bernie, and this room and its contents would remain unaffected. It is one enormous fire-safe."

"But if the fire broke out in here…"

"How? I don't smoke, or play with matches. There are no cupboards holding piles of oily rags, no bales of moldering hay to burst into spontaneous combustion."

"No, but—"

"And even if there were a fire," he said, "it would be extinguished almost before it had begun." He gestured and I looked up and saw round metal gadgets spotted here and there in the walls and ceiling.

I said, "A sprinkler system? Somebody tried to sell me one at the store once and I threw him out on his ear. Fire's rough on books, but water's sheer disaster. And those things are like smoke alarms, they can go off for no good reason, and then where are you? Karl, I can't believe—"

"Please," he said, holding up a hand. "Do you take me for an idiot?"

"No, but—"

"Do you honestly think I would use water to forestall fire? Credit me with a little sense, my friend."

"I do, but—"

"There will be no fire here, and no flood, either. A book in my library will be, ah, what is the expression? Snug as a slug in a rug."

"A bug," I said.

"I beg your pardon?"

"A bug in a rug," I said. "I think that's the expression."

His response was a shrug, the sort you'd get, I suppose, from a slug in a rug. "But we have no time for language lessons," he said. "From two to six I must be in the library with my books, and it is already one-fifty."

"You're already in the library."

"Alone," he said. "With only my books for company. So. What have you brought me?"

I opened my briefcase, withdrew the padded mailer, reached into that like Little Jack Horner and brought forth a plum indeed. I looked up in time to catch an unguarded glimpse of Bellermann's face, and it was a study. How often do you get to see a man salivate less than an hour after a big lunch?

He extended his hands and I placed the book in them. "*Fer-de-Lance*," he said reverently. "Nero Wolfe's debut, the rarest and most desirable book in the entire canon. Hardly the best of the novels, I wouldn't say. It took Stout several books fully to refine the character of Wolfe and to hone the narrative edge of Archie Goodwin. But the brilliance was present from the beginning, and the book is a prize."

He turned the volume over in his hands, inspected the dust jacket fore and aft. "Of course I own a copy," he said. "A first edition in dust wrapper. This dust wrapper is nicer than the one I have."

"It's pretty cherry," I said.

"Pristine," he allowed, "or very nearly so. Mine has a couple of chips and an unfortunate tear mended quite expertly with tape. This does look virtually perfect."

"Yes."

"But the jacket's the least of it, is it not? This is a special copy."

"It is."

He opened it, and his large hands could not have been gentler had he been repotting orchids. He found the title page and read, "'For Franklin Roosevelt, with the earnest hope of a brighter tomorrow. Best regards from Rex Todhunter Stout.'" He ran his forefinger over the inscription. "It's Stout's writing," he announced. "He didn't inscribe many books, but I have enough signed copies to know his hand. And this is the ultimate association copy, isn't it?"

"You could say that."

"I just did. Stout was a liberal Democrat, ultimately a World Federalist. FDR, like the present incumbent, was a great fan of detective stories. It always seems to be the Democratic presidents who relish a good mystery. Eisenhower preferred Westerns, Nixon liked history and biography, and I don't know that Reagan read at all."

He sighed and closed the book. "Mr. Gulbenkian must regret the loss of this copy," he said.

"I suppose he must."

"A year ago," he said, "when I learned he'd been burglarized and some of his best volumes stolen, I wondered what sort of burglar could possibly know what books to take. And of course I thought of you."

I didn't say anything.

"Tell me your price again, Bernie. Refresh my memory."

I named a figure.

"It's high," he said.

"The book's unique," I pointed out.

"I know that. I know, too, that I can never show it off. I cannot tell anyone I have it. You and I alone will know that it is in my possession."

"It'll be our little secret, Karl."

"Our little secret. I can't even insure it. At least Gulbenkian was insured, eh? But he can never replace the book. Why didn't you sell it back to him?"

"I might," I said, "if you decide you don't want it."

"But of course I want it!" He might have said more but a glance at his watch reminded him of the time. "Two o'clock," he said, motioning me toward the door. "Eva will have my afternoon coffee ready. And you will excuse me, I am sure, while I spend the afternoon with my books, including this latest specimen."

"Be careful with it," I said.

"Bernie! I'm not going to *read* it. I have plenty of reading copies, should I care to renew my acquaintance with *Fer-de-Lance*. I want to hold it, to be with it. And then at six o'clock we will conclude our business, and I will give you a dinner every bit as good as the lunch you just had. And then you can return to the city."

HE USHERED me out, and moments later he disappeared into the library again, carrying a tray with coffee in one of those silver pots they used to give you on trains. There was a cup on the tray as well, and a sugar bowl and creamer, along with a plate of shortbread cookies. I stood in the hall and watched the library door swing shut, heard the lock turn and the bolt slide home. Then I turned, and there was Karl's wife, Eva.

"I guess he's really going to spend the next four hours in there," I said. "He always does."

"I'd go for a drive," I said, "but I don't have a car. I suppose I could go for a walk. It's a beautiful day, bright and sunny. Of course your husband doesn't allow sunlight into the library, but I suppose he lets it go where it wants in the rest of the neighborhood."

That drew a smile from her.

"If I'd thought ahead," I said, "I'd have brought something to read. Not that there aren't a few thousand books in the house, but they're all locked away with Karl."

"Not all of them," she said. "My husband's collection is limited to books published before 1975, along with the more recent work of a few of his very favorite authors. But he buys other contemporary crime novels as well, and keeps them here and there around the house. The bookcase in the guest room is well stocked."

"That's good news. As far as that goes, I was in the middle of a magazine story."

"In *Ellery Queen*, wasn't it? Come with me, Mr. Rhodenbarr, and I'll—"

"Bernie."

"Bernie," she said, and colored slightly, those dangerous cheekbones turning from ivory to the pink you find inside a seashell. "I'll show you where the guest room is, Bernie, and then I'll bring you your magazine."

The guest room was on the second floor, and its glassed-in bookcase was indeed jam-packed with recent crime fiction. I was just getting drawn into the opening of one of Jeremiah Healy's Cuddy novels when Eva Bellermann knocked on the half-open door and came in with a tray quite like the one she'd brought her husband. Coffee in a silver pot, a gold-rimmed bone china cup and saucer, a matching plate holding short-bread cookies. And, keeping them company, the issue of EQMM I'd been reading earlier.

"This is awfully nice of you," I said. "But you should have brought a second cup so you could join me."

"I've had too much coffee already," she said. "But I could keep you company for a few minutes if you don't mind."

"I'd like that."

"So would I," she said, skirting my chair and sitting on the edge of the narrow captain's bed. "I don't get much company. The people in the village keep their distance. And Karl has his books."

"And he's locked away with them…"

"Three hours in the morning and four in the afternoon. Then in the evening he deals with correspondence and returns phone calls. He's retired, as you know, but he has investment decisions to make and business matters to deal with. And books, of course. He's always buying more of them." She sighed. "I'm afraid he doesn't have much time left for me."

"It must be difficult for you."

"It's lonely," she said.

"I can imagine."

"We have so little in common," she said. "I sometimes wonder why he married me. The books are his whole life."

"And they don't interest you at all?"

She shook her head. "I haven't the brain for it," she said. "Clues and timetables and elaborate murder methods. It is like working a crossword puzzle without a pencil. Or worse—like assembling a jigsaw puzzle in the dark."

"With gloves on," I suggested.

"Oh, that's funny!" She laughed more than the line warranted and laid a hand on my arm. "But I should not make jokes about the books. You are a bookseller yourself. Perhaps books are your whole life, too."

"Not my whole life," I said.

"Oh? What else interests you?"

"Beautiful women," I said recklessly.

"Beautiful women?"

"Like you," I said.

BELIEVE ME, I hadn't planned on any of this. I'd figured on finishing the Lovesey story, then curling up with the Healy book until Karl Bellermann emerged from his lair, saw his shadow, and paid me a lot of money for the book he thought I had stolen.

In point of fact, the *Fer-de-Lance* I'd brought him was legitimately mine to sell—or very nearly so. I would never have entertained the notion of breaking into Nizar Gulbenkian's fieldstone house in Riverdale. Gulbenkian was a friend as well as a valued customer, and I'd rushed to call him when I learned of his loss. I would keep an ear cocked and an eye open, I assured him, and I would let him know if any of his treasures turned up on the gray or black market.

"That's kind of you, Bernie," he'd said. "We will have to talk of this one day."

And, months later, we talked—and I learned there had been no burglary. Gulbenkian had gouged his own front door with a chisel, looted his own well-insured library of its greatest treasures, and tucked them out of sight (if not out of mind) before reporting the offense—and pocketing the payoff from the insurance company.

He'd needed money, of course, and this had seemed a good way to get it without parting with his precious volumes. But now he needed more money, as one so often does, and he had a carton full of books he no longer legally owned and could not even show off to his friends, let alone display to the public. He couldn't offer them for sale, either, but someone else could. Someone who might be presumed to have stolen them. Someone rather like me.

"It will be the simplest thing in the world for you, Bernie," old Nizar said. "You won't have to do any breaking or entering. You won't even have to come to Riverdale. All you'll do is sell the books, and I will gladly pay you ten percent of the proceeds."

"Half," I said.

We settled on a third, after protracted negotiations, and later over drinks he allowed that he'd have gone as high as forty percent, while I admitted I'd have taken twenty. He brought me the books, and I knew which one to offer first, and to whom.

The FDR *Fer-de-Lance* was the prize of the lot, and the most readily identifiable. Karl Bellermann was likely to pay the highest price for it, and to be most sanguine about its unorthodox provenance.

You hear it said of a man now and then that he'd rather steal a dollar than earn ten. (It's been said, not entirely without justification, of me.)

Karl Bellermann was a man who'd rather buy a stolen book for a thousand dollars than pay half that through legitimate channels. I'd sold him things in the past, some stolen, some not, and it was the volume with a dubious history that really got him going.

So, as far as he was concerned, I'd lifted *Fer-de-Lance* from its rightful owner, who would turn purple if he knew where it was. But I knew better—Gulbenkian would cheerfully pocket two-thirds of whatever I pried out of Bellermann, and would know exactly where the book had wound up and just how it got there.

In a sense, then, I was putting one over on Karl Bellermann, but that didn't constitute a breach of my admittedly elastic moral code. It was something else entirely, though, to abuse the man's hospitality by putting the moves on his gorgeous young wife.

Well, what can I say? Nobody's perfect.

AFTERWARD I lay back with my head on a pillow and tried to figure out what would make a man choose a leather chair and a room full of books over a comfortable bed with a hot blonde in it. I marveled at the vagaries of human nature, and Eva stroked my chest and urged a cup of coffee on me.

It was great coffee, and no less welcome after our little interlude. The cookies were good, too. Eva took one, but passed on the coffee. If she drank it after lunchtime, she said, she had trouble sleeping nights.

"It never keeps me awake," I said. "In fact, this stuff seems to be having just the opposite effect. The more I drink, the sleepier I get."

"Maybe it is I who have made you sleepy."

"Could be."

She snuggled close, letting interesting parts of her body press against mine. "Perhaps we should close our eyes for a few minutes," she said.

The next thing I knew she had a hand on my shoulder and was shaking me awake. "Bernie," she said. "We fell asleep!"

"We did?"

"And look at the time! It is almost six o'clock. Karl will be coming out of the library any minute."

"Uh-oh."

She was out of bed, diving into her clothes. "I'll go downstairs," she said. "You can take your time dressing, as long as we are not together." And, before I could say anything, she swept out of the room.

I had the urge to close my eyes and drift right off again. Instead I forced myself out of bed, took a quick shower to clear the cobwebs, then got dressed. I stood for a moment at the head of the stairs, listening for conversation and hoping I wouldn't hear any voices raised in anger. I didn't hear any voices, angry or otherwise, or anything else.

It's quiet out there, I thought, like so many supporting characters in so many Westerns. And the thought came back, as it had from so many heroes in those same Westerns: *Yeah...too quiet.*

I descended the flight of stairs, turned a corner and bumped into Eva. "He hasn't come out," she said. "Bernie, I'm worried."

"Maybe he lost track of the time."

"Never. He's like a Swiss watch, and he *has* a Swiss watch and checks it constantly. He comes out every day at six on the dot. It is ten minutes past the hour and where is he?"

"Maybe he came out and—"

"Yes?"

"I don't know. Drove into town to buy a paper."

"He never does that. And the car is in the garage."

"He could have gone for a walk."

"He hates to walk. Bernie, he is still in there."

"Well, I suppose he's got the right. It's his room and his books. If he wants to hang around—"

"I'm afraid something has happened to him. Bernie, I knocked on the door. I knocked loud. Perhaps you heard the sound upstairs?"

"No, but I probably wouldn't. I was all the way upstairs, and I had the shower on for a while there. I take it he didn't answer."

"No."

"Well, I gather it's pretty well soundproofed in there. Maybe he didn't hear you."

"I have knocked before. And he has heard me before."

"Maybe he heard you this time and decided to ignore you." Why was I raising so many objections? Perhaps because I didn't want to let myself think there was any great cause for alarm.

"Bernie," she said, "what if he is ill? What if he has had a heart attack?"

"I suppose it's possible, but—"

"I think I should call the police."

I suppose it's my special perspective, but I almost never think that's a great idea. I wasn't mad about it now, either, being in the possession of stolen property and a criminal record, not to mention the guilty conscience that I'd earned a couple of hours ago in the upstairs guest room.

"Not the police," I said. "Not yet. First let's make sure he's not just taking a nap, or all caught up in his reading."

"But how? The door is locked."

"Isn't there an extra key?"

"If there is, he's never told me where he keeps it. He's the only one with access to his precious books."

"The window," I said.

"It can't be opened. It is this triple pane of bulletproof glass, and—"

"And you couldn't budge it with a battering ram," I said. "He told me all about it. You can still see through it, though, can't you?"

"HE'S IN there," I announced. "At least his feet are."

"His feet?"

"There's a big leather chair with its back to the window," I said, "and he's sitting in it. I can't see the rest of him, but I can see his feet."

"What are they doing?"

"They're sticking out in front of the chair," I said, "and they're wearing shoes, and that's about it. Feet aren't terribly expressive, are they?"

I made a fist and reached up to bang on the window. I don't know what I expected the feet to do in response, but they stayed right where they were.

"The police," Eva said. "I'd better call them."

"Not just yet," I said.

THE POULARD is a terrific lock, no question about it. State-of-the-art and all that. But I don't know where they get off calling it pickproof. When I first came across the word in one of their ads I knew how Alexander felt when he heard about the Gordian knot. Pickproof, eh? We'll see about that!

The lock on the library door put up a good fight, but I'd brought the little set of picks and probes I never leave home without, and I put them (and my God-given talent) to the task.

And opened the door.

"Bernie," Eva said, gaping. "Where did you learn how to do that?"

"In the Boy Scouts," I said. "They give you a merit badge for it if you apply yourself. Karl? Karl, are you all right?"

He was in his chair, and now we could see more than his well-shod feet. His hands were in his lap, holding a book by William Campbell Gault. His head was back, his eyes closed. He looked for all the world like a man who'd dozed off over a book.

We stood looking at him, and I took a moment to sniff the air. I'd smelled something on my first visit to this remarkable room, but I couldn't catch a whiff of it now.

"Bernie—"

I looked down, scanned the floor, running my eyes over the maroon broadloom and the carpets that covered most of it. I dropped to one knee alongside one small Persian—a Tabriz, if I had to guess, but I know less than a good burglar should about the subject. I took a close look at this one and Eva asked me what I was doing.

"Just helping out," I said. "Didn't you drop a contact lens?"

"I don't wear contact lenses."

"My mistake," I said, and got to my feet. I went over to the big leather chair and went through the formality of laying a hand on Karl Bellermann's brow. It was predictably cool to the touch.

"Is he—"

I nodded. "You'd better call the cops," I said.

ELMER CRITTENDEN, the officer in charge, was a stocky fellow in a khaki windbreaker. He kept glancing warily at the walls of books, as if he feared being called upon to sit down and read them one after the other. My guess is that he'd had less experience with them than with dead bodies.

"Most likely turn out to be his heart," he said of the deceased. "Usually is when they go like this. He complain any of chest pains? Shooting pains up and down his left arm? Any of that?"

Eva said he hadn't.

"Might have had 'em without saying anything," Crittenden said. "Or it could be he didn't get any advance warning. Way he's sitting and all, I'd say it was quick. Could be he closed his eyes for a little nap and died in his sleep."

"Just so he didn't suffer," Eva said.

Crittenden lifted Karl's eyelid, squinted, touched the corpse here and there. "What it almost looks like," he said, "is that he was smothered, but I don't suppose some great speckled bird flew in a window and held a pillow over his face. It'll turn out to be a heart attack, unless I miss my guess."

Could I just let it go? I looked at Crittenden, at Eva, at the sunburst pattern on the high ceiling up above, at the putative Tabriz carpet below. Then I looked at Karl, the consummate bibliophile, with FDR's *Fer-de-Lance* on the table beside his chair. He was my customer, and he'd died within arm's reach of the book I'd brought him. Should I let him *requiescat* in relative *pace*? Or did I have an active role to play?

"I think you were right," I told Crittenden. "I think he was smothered."

"What would make you say that, sir? You didn't even get a good look at his eyeballs."

"I'll trust your eyeballs," I said. "And I don't think it was a great speckled bird that did it, either."

"Oh?"

"It's classic," I said, "and it would have appealed to Karl, given his passion for crime fiction. If he had to die, he'd probably have wanted it to happen in a locked room. And not just any locked room, either, but one secured by a pickproof Poulard, with steel-lined walls and windows that don't open."

"He was locked up tighter than Fort Knox," Crittenden said.

"He was," I said. "And, all the same, he was murdered."

"SMOTHERED," I said. "When the lab checks him out, tell them to look for Halon gas. I think it'll show up, but not unless they're looking for it."

"I never heard of it," Crittenden said.

"Most people haven't," I said. "It was in the news a while ago when they installed it in subway toll booths. There'd been a few incendiary attacks on booth attendants—a spritz of something flammable and they got turned into crispy critters. The Halon gas was there to smother a fire before it got started."

"How's it work?"

"It displaces the oxygen in the room," I said. "I'm not enough of a scientist to know how it manages it, but the net effect is about the same as that great speckled bird you were talking about. The one with the pillows."

"That'd be consistent with the physical evidence," Crittenden said. "But how would you get this Halon in here?"

"It was already here," I said. I pointed to the jets on the walls and ceiling. "When I first saw them, I thought Bellermann had put in a conventional sprinkler system, and I couldn't believe it. Water's harder than fire on rare books, and a lot of libraries have been totaled when a sprinkler system went off by accident. I said something to that effect to Karl, and he just about bit my head off, making it clear he wouldn't expose his precious treasures to water damage.

"So I got the picture. The jets were designed to deliver gas, not liquid, and it went without saying that the gas would be Halon. I understand they're equipping the better research libraries with it these days, although Karl's the only person I know of who installed it in his personal library."

Crittenden was halfway up a ladder, having a look at one of the outlets. "Just like a sprinkler head," he said, "which is what I took it for. How's it know when to go off? Heat sensor?"

"That's right."

"You said murder. That'd mean somebody set it off."

"Yes."

"By starting a fire in here? Be a neater trick than sending in the great speckled bird."

"All you'd have to do," I said, "is heat the sensor enough to trigger the response."

"How?"

"When I was in here earlier," I said, "I caught a whiff of smoke. It was faint, but it was absolutely there. I think that's what made me ask Karl about fire in the first place."

"And?"

"When Mrs. Bellermann and I came in and discovered the body, the smell was gone. But there was a discolored spot on the carpet that I'd noticed before, and I bent down for a closer look at it." I pointed to the Tabriz (which, now that I think about it, may very well have been an Isfahan). "Right there," I said.

Crittenden knelt where I pointed, rubbed two fingers on the spot, brought them to his nose. "Scorched," he reported. "But just the least bit. Take a whole lot more than that to set off a sensor way up there."

"I know. That was a test."

"A test?"

"Of the murder method. How do you raise the temperature of a room you can't enter? You can't unlock the door and you can't open the window. How can you get enough heat in to set off the gas?"

"How?"

I turned to Eva. "Tell him how you did it," I said.

"I don't know what you're talking about," she said. "You must be crazy."

"You wouldn't need a fire," I said. "You wouldn't even need a whole lot of heat. All you'd have to do is deliver enough heat directly to the sensor to trigger a response. If you could manage that in a highly localized fashion, you wouldn't even raise the overall room temperature appreciably."

"Keep talking," Crittenden said.

I picked up an ivory-handled magnifier, one of several placed strategically around the room. "When I was a Boy Scout," I said, "they didn't really teach me how to open locks. But they were big on starting fires. Flint and steel, fire by friction—and that old standby, focusing the sun's rays through a magnifying glass and delivering a concentrated pinpoint of intense heat onto something with a low kindling point."

"The window," Crittenden said.

I nodded. "It faces north," I said, "so the sun never comes in on its own. But you can stand a few feet from the window and catch the sunlight with a mirror, and you can tilt the mirror so the light is reflected through your magnifying glass and on through the window. And you can beam it onto an object in the room."

"The heat sensor, that'd be."

"Eventually," I said. "First, though, you'd want to make sure it would work. You couldn't try it out ahead of time on the sensor, because you wouldn't know it was working until you set it off. Until then, you couldn't be sure the thickness of the window glass wasn't disrupting the process. So you'd want to test it."

"That explains the scorched rug, doesn't it?" Crittenden stooped for another look at it, then glanced up at the window. "Soon as you saw a wisp of smoke or a trace of scorching, you'd know it was working. And you'd have an idea how long it would take to raise the temperature enough. If you could make it hot enough to scorch wool, you could set off a heat-sensitive alarm."

"My God," Eva cried, adjusting quickly to new realities. "I thought you must be crazy, but now I can see how it was done. But who could have done such a thing?"

"Oh, I don't know," I said. "I suppose it would have to be somebody who lived here, somebody who was familiar with the library and knew about the Halon, somebody who stood to gain financially by Karl Bellermann's death. Somebody, say, who felt neglected by a husband who treated her like a housekeeper, somebody who might see poetic justice in killing him while he was locked away with his precious books."

"You can't mean me, Bernie."

"Well, now that you mention it..."

"But I was with you! Karl was with us at lunch. Then he went into the library and I showed you to the guest room."

"You showed me, all right."

"And we were together," she said, lowering her eyes modestly. "It shames me to say it with my husband tragically dead, but we were in bed

89

together until almost six o'clock, when we came down here to discover the body. You can testify to that, can't you, Bernie?"

"I can swear we went to bed together," I said, "And I can swear that *I* was there until six, unless I went sleepwalking. But I was out cold, Eva."

"So was I."

"I don't think so," I said. "You stayed away from the coffee, saying how it kept you awake. Well, it sure didn't keep *me* awake. I think there was something in it to make me sleep, and that's why you didn't want any. I think there was more of the same in the pot you gave Karl to bring in here with him, so he'd be dozing peacefully while you set off the Halon. You waited until I was asleep, went outside with a mirror and a magnifier, heated the sensor and set off the gas, and then came back to bed. The Halon would do its work in minutes, and without warning even if Karl wasn't sleeping all that soundly. Halon's odorless and colorless, and the air cleaning system would whisk it all away in less than an hour. But I think there'll be traces in his system, along with traces of the same sedative they'll find in the residue in both the coffee pots. And I think that'll be enough to put you away."

Crittenden thought so, too.

WHEN I got back to the city there was a message on the machine to call Nizar Gulbenkian. It was late, but it sounded urgent.

"Bad news," I told him. "I had the book just about sold. Then he locked himself in his library to commune with the ghosts of Rex Stout and Franklin Delano Roosevelt, and next thing he knew they were all hanging out together."

"You don't mean he died?"

"His wife killed him," I said, and I went on to tell him the whole story. "So that's the bad news, though it's not as bad for us as it is for the Bellermanns. I've got the book back, and I'm sure I can find a customer for it."

"Ah," he said. "Well, Bernie, I'm sorry about Bellermann. He was a true bookman."

"He was that, all right."

"But otherwise your bad news is good news."

"It is?"

"Yes. Because I changed my mind about the book."

"You don't want to sell it?"

"I *can't* sell it," he said. "It would be like tearing out my soul. And now, thank God, I don't have to sell it."

"Oh?"

"More good news," he said. "A business transaction, a long shot with a handsome return. I won't bore you with the details, but the outcome was very good indeed. If you'd been successful in selling the book, I'd now be begging you to buy it back."

"I see."

"Bernie," he said, "I'm a collector, as passionate about the pursuit as poor Bellermann. I don't ever want to sell. I want to add to my holdings." He let out a sigh, clearly pleased at the prospect. "So I'll want the book back. But of course I'll pay you your commission all the same."

"I couldn't accept it."

"So you had all that work for nothing?"

"Not exactly," I said.

"Oh?"

"I guess Bellermann's library will go on the auction block eventually," I said. "Eva can't inherit, but there'll be some niece or nephew to wind up with a nice piece of change. And there'll be some wonderful books in that sale."

"There certainly will."

"But a few of the most desirable items won't be included," I said, "because they somehow found their way into my briefcase, along with *Fer-de-Lance*."

"You managed that, Bernie? With a dead body in the room, and a murderer in custody, and a cop right there on the scene?"

"Bellermann had shown me his choicest treasures," I said, "so I knew just what to grab and where to find it. And Crittenden didn't care what I did with the books. I told him I needed something to read on the train and he waited patiently while I picked out eight or ten volumes. Well, it's a long train ride, and I guess he must think I'm a fast reader."

"Bring them over," he said. "Now."

"Nizar, I'm bushed," I said, "and you're all the way up in Riverdale. First thing in the morning, okay? And while I'm there you can teach me how to tell a Tabriz from an Isfahan."

"They're not at all alike, Bernie. How could anyone confuse them?"

"You'll clear it up for me tomorrow. Okay?"

"Well, all right," he said. "But I hate to wait."

Collectors! Don't you just love them?

THE BURGLAR WHO COLLECTED COPERNICUS

RAY KIRSCHMANN, THE BEST cop money can buy, found his way between the piles of books and leaned on my counter. "Bern," he said, "this Coppernickels thing's got your fingerprints all over it."

"Coppernickels?"

"Polish guy with a telescope. Said the earth revolves around the sun, which every kid in school knows, so what's the big deal?"

"Copernicus," I said. "I think he said it first."

"Wrote a whole book about it, Bern. There's 260 of 'em left in the whole world, and each one's worth 400 grand. And somebody's stealing 'em."

"I read about it," I said carefully. "Here's something to think about, Ray. If you multiply it out, the world's supply of *De Revolutionibus Orbium Coelestium* is worth $94 million, and the distance between the earth and the sun is 93 million miles."

"Bern—"

"Coincidence, Ray? I don't think so."

He gave me a look. "There's seven books been stolen so far," he said, "minimum. Swiped out of libraries and colleges all over the world. In Kiev the thief posed as a cop."

"Imagine that," I said.

"Bern," he said, "when I fire up the old mental computer and punch in 'old books' and 'grand larceny,' what always comes up is Bernie Rhodenbarr."

"Maybe you should upgrade," I suggested. "Maybe it's a software problem. Ray, why would anyone want to steal Copernicus? You couldn't turn around and sell it. And, even if you did have a customer, some rich collector who'd keep it in his safe and never show it to anybody, one copy's all he'd want. Nobody in his right mind would try to steal all of them."

I don't think I convinced him, but eventually he went off to enforce the law somewhere else. And the next person through the door was my new best friend, Evan Tanner. "You're up early," I said.

He gave me a look. Tanner hasn't slept since a shard of North Korean shrapnel destroyed the sleep center of his brain. That would make him somewhere in his sixties, but he spent a quarter of a century in a frozen food locker and looks about forty.

"Copernicus," he said heavily, and started going on about plano-terrestrialism and the globularist heresy. Tanner's a member of the Flat Earth Society.

"Heliocentrism has to be stamped out," he said. "A flat earth at the center of the Universe, that's what we need if we're going to feel comfortable about ourselves. Well, Rhodenbarr? Do you have the book?"

A BURGLAR'S-EYE
VIEW OF GREED

SO I WALKED OVER to Barnegat Books on East
Eleventh Street for a word with my favorite bookseller,
Bernie Rhodenbarr. He was behind the counter with his
nose in a book while his cat lay in the window, soaking up the sun. The
store's sole customer was a young woman with multiple piercings who was
reading a biography of St. Sebastian.

"I understand the used-book business is hot these days," I said. "You
must be making money hand over fist."

He gave me a look. "Every now and then," he said, "somebody actually
buys a book. It's a good thing I don't have to depend on this place to keep
body and soul together."

He doesn't have to pay rent, either, having bought the building with
the profits from his other career as the last of the gentleman burglars.
Seriously, I told him, lots of people were making big bucks selling books on
the Internet. Couldn't he do the same?

"I could," he agreed. "I could list my entire stock on eBay and spend my
time wrapping books and schlepping them to the Post Office. I could close
the store, because who needs a retail outlet when you've got a computer
and a modem? But I didn't open this store to get rich. I opened it so I could
have a bookstore, and have fun running it, and occasionally meet girls.
See, I'm not greedy."

"But you steal," I pointed out.

He frowned, and nodded toward St. Sebastian's biggest fan. "Not to get rich," he said. "Only enough to get by. I don't want to get rich, see, because it would turn me into a greedy pig."

"You're saying the rich are greedy?"

"They don't necessarily start out that way," he said, "but that's how it seems to work. Look at all the CEOs with their eight-figure salaries. The more you pay them, the more they want, and when the company goes down the tubes they float down on their golden parachute and look for another corporation to sink. Or look at baseball."

"Baseball?"

"America's pastime," he said. "The players used to have off-season jobs so they could make ends meet. The owners were always rich guys, but they were in it for the sport. They didn't expect to make money."

"And?"

"And now the players average something like two million dollars a year, and the owners have watched their investments increase in value by a factor of five or ten, and everybody's rich, so everybody's greedy. And that's why we're going to have a strike this fall. Because they're all pigs, and all they want is more."

"In other words," I said, "success turns men to swine."

"And women," he said. "Success is an equal-opportunity corrupter. And it seems to be inevitable nowadays. Nobody's happy just running a business and making a living. Everybody wants to grow the business, and either franchise it or sell it to a huge corporation. Luckily, I'm safe. Nobody's aching to franchise Barnegat Books, and no multinational corporation's trying to buy me out."

"So you'll go on selling books."

"Every now and then," he said, as the young woman put St. Sebastian back on the shelf and walked away empty-handed. "I'll tell you, it's a good thing I'm a thief. It keeps me honest."

THE BURGLAR
ON LOCATION

SO I AMBLED OVER to Barnegat Books on East
Eleventh to get Bernie Rhodenbarr's spin on the proposed real estate legislation. It was lunchtime, and my
favorite burglar and his buddy, Carolyn Kaiser, were all set to tuck into the
blue plate special from the Laotian joint around the corner. Raffles the Cat
was in the fiction section, stalking imaginary mice.

"When I sell somebody a book," Bernie said, "I'm under no obligation
to tell the buyer who owned it last."

"Sometimes you don't have to," Carolyn pointed out. "If there's a book-
plate. Or if it's from a library."

"Any ex-library copy in this store," he said icily, "is stamped
WITHDRAWN."

I didn't ask him where he kept the stamp. "Some people would argue
that real estate's a little different," I said. "Nobody lives in a book."

"Oh?"

"If you were going to buy a house," I said, "or move into an apartment,
wouldn't you want to know if something horrible happened there?"

"This is New York," he said. "Something horrible's happened everywhere."

"It's true," Carolyn said. "This store, for instance. Remember when we
found the dead guy in the john?"

"Edwin Turnquist. A guy named Jacobi killed him and left him there."

"And then we put him in a wheelchair and left him over by the river," Carolyn recalled. "It was sort of like a granny-dumping, except he was already dead. And how about the carriage house on West 18th where Wanda Colcannon was murdered? Or Abel Crowe's place on Riverside Drive, where the podiatrist killed him?"

"Or East 67th Street, where J. Francis Flaxford was bludgeoned," he said. "Or Gramercy Park, where Crystal Sheldrake was stabbed with one of her husband's dental scalpels. Or the Nugents' apartment on West End, where I found Luke Santangelo dead in the bathtub. Or Gordon Onderdonk's apartment at the Charlemagne, or Hugo Candlemas's floor-through at 76th and Lex."

"Remember Walter Grabow, Bernie? Killed right in your apartment."

"Thanks for reminding me," he said. "But that's the point, isn't it? Even ordinary people like us can point to residences all over town where violent scenes have taken place."

"Like the argument I had with Randy Messinger at my place on Arbor Court," she said. "We were yelling at the top of our lungs." She shuddered at the memory. "But you're right, and think of the other murder sites we know about. The hotel where Kim Dakkinen was chopped to bits with a machete in *Eight Million Ways to Die*. The Bethune Street apartment where Wendy Hanniford was knifed in *The Sins of the Fathers*. The house in Sunset Park where Kenan Khoury caught up with his wife's killer."

"And what about the arena in Maspeth, where Matt and Mick Ballou faced off against Borden and Olga Stettner?"

"Wait a minute," I said. "Those are all books about Matthew Scudder. They're novels."

"So?"

"They're fiction," I said. "Don't you know the difference?"

He shrugged. "Does anybody? Besides, this is New York. Everybody knows New York's not about fact or fiction. New York's about real estate. The facts don't matter."

"Then what does?"

Raffles the Cat leapt gracefully, demolishing a fictional mouse.

"Three things," my larcenous friend said. "Location, location and location."

FIVE BOOKS
BERNIE HAS READ
MORE THAN ONCE

I **GET TO DO** a lot of reading on the job. (No, not the job that involves breaking and entering. I'm talking about my day job, selling pre-owned works of literature at Barnegat Books on East Eleventh Street in Greenwich Village.) Far too many of those diurnal hours are spent with only my cat for company, so I usually have a book at hand when I'm otherwise unoccupied behind the counter.

Much of the time, it's a book I've read before, and sometimes more than once. There's a great comfort in settling down with a novel I know I'll enjoy—because I've already done so. But not every book that's a pleasure the first time around is going to wear well on a second visit.

Here are five—now how did I come up with that number?—that never let me down:

1. The Parker series, by Donald E. Westlake writing as Richard Stark. The University of Chicago Press has just reissued the complete series in trade paperback, and that's a good thing, because my own copies have fallen apart from frequent rereading. Do I like Parker because he's a thief? Well, I'm sure that's part of his charm, but I just plain like the way Parker thinks and acts and reacts, and the way Richard Stark writes.

Westlake wrote another wonderful series about a gang of criminals led by a remarkably hapless chap named John Dortmunder, and those are wonderful, too, but I don't find myself returning to them the same way. The Parker books are self-contained, but it's best to start with *The Hunter* (the basis for the great Lee Marvin film *Point Blank*) and read them in order. Of course, when you're rereading, you've been here before—so you can feel free to skip around.

2. Thomas Flanagan's *The Year of the French*. Flanagan wrote three wonderful historical novels set in Ireland. This one takes place in 1798, when Ireland rose in revolt—in Wexford ("But the gold sun of freedom grew darkened at Ross / And it set by the Slaney's red waves / And poor Wexford, stripped naked, hung high on the cross / With her heart pierced by traitors and slaves. / Glory-o Glory-o for the bold men who died / For the sake of long downtrodden man! / Glory-o to Mount Leinster's own darlin' and pride / Dauntless Kelly, the boy from Killane!") and Dublin and in the West. ("So here's to the gallant old West / Where hearts are the bravest and best / When Ireland lay broken in Wexford / Hurrah for the men of the West!")

I only like historical fiction when it's wonderful, and this one is. As with the greatest tragedy, one keeps revisiting it in the hope that this time round it'll have a happy ending. But, as Elaine Scudder observed of La Boheme, "She always dies. How many times have I seen that opera? Mimi dies every @#$%^!! time." Parts Two and Three of the trilogy, *The Tenants of Time* and *The End of the Hunt*, are also great books, but not as easy to get into.

3. *The Queen's Gambit* by Walter Tevis. There are books that are not mysteries, not genre fiction in any sense, yet they have a strong following among people who read mysteries. The late Carol Bremer of Murder Ink had a section of non-mysteries she recommended to readers. Kinsella's *Shoeless Joe* was one I recall finding there, and this wonderful novel was another.

The heroine is a chess prodigy, and the drama's conducted largely over a chessboard, and you don't have to know a knight and a bishop from Adam's off ox in order to find every page gripping and engrossing. I've read it several times and am about ready to read it again.

4. John Sandford's books about Lucas Davenport are a richer experience the second time around. They're so riveting, so suspenseful, that my

only interest the first time around is to see what happens next. So I tear through the book and love it, but I miss a lot—and the books are sufficiently textured to make a second look rewarding. I was well into the series before I could begin to tell Davenport's fellow cops apart, or care which one of them was riding shotgun.

A year or so ago I re-read the whole series, starting with *Rules of Prey*, and the books were still riveting (especially the two about Clara Rinker, who can park her shoes under this burglar's bed anytime she wants to). But they were richer, too, and I got a lot more out of them. During *The Burglar on the Prowl* I was reading the one about a disillusioned ex-vegetarian Congregationalist minister making his brutal way around Minnesota, slaughtering prominent vegans and organic farmers, butchering them, and eating their livers. Have you read that one yet? Carolyn liked the title, too: *Lettuce Prey.*

5. Some of you have noticed that I don't look a day older than I did at my debut 36 years ago in *Burglars Can't Be Choosers.* That's one of the joys of being a fictional character. You get to be the same age forever. (Unless the person chronicling your existence is the kind of killjoy who insists on aging you in real time. That's what happened to Matthew Scudder, the poor bastard.) But not I, and not either of Agatha Christie's brightest stars, Hercule Poirot and Miss Jane Marple.

Poirot was an elderly retired Belgian detective in his (and Dame Agatha's) debut in *The Mysterious Affair at Styles*, back in 1920; when his curtain came down with *Curtain* in 1975, well, he wasn't any younger, but he wasn't any older either.

And the same can be said for Miss Marple, who like Poirot starred in a long run of superbly crafted mysteries. I think I've read them all, and I've read many of them more than once, especially the Marples, because I find her continually interesting. I always found Poirot to be a stick festooned with mannerisms, and I find it astonishing that someone's going to revive Poirot and write a new novel about him. Why, for the love of Dieu? Without Christie's plotting, what would you have? Marple's different, but even so, I don't see much point in bringing her back. If you want to revive somebody, figure out a way to bring Agatha Christie back to life. Failing that, reread the books. There's always a good supply of them at Barnegat Books.

101

A BURGLAR'S COMPLAINT

SO I TOOK THE subway to Union Square and walked a couple of blocks to a storefront on East Eleventh Street, where a tailless cat dozed in the window. Inside I found Bernie Rhodenbarr perched on a stool behind the counter, reading the latest Wallace Stroby novel.

"It's about Crissa Stone," my favorite bookseller announced. "A professional thief. Sort of like Richard Stark's Parker, but without a Y chromosome. I'll tell you, it makes me miss the old days."

"When men were men?"

"When it was possible for an enterprising individual to make money the old-fashioned way."

"By working for it?"

He shook his head. "By stealing it. And I'm not talking about computer crime and identity theft and all of that sneaky cyber-stuff. I mean leaving one's own house and letting oneself into somebody else's. I mean breaking and entering—and then exiting, richer than when you entered. I mean picking locks and jimmying doors and outfoxing doormen and elevator operators."

"You mean burglary."

"Once," he said, "it was a profession. A morally reprehensible one, I'll grant you, but one with a set of standards and a code of ethics and a steep learning curve, designed to separate the sheep from the goats, the ribbon from the clerks, and the fool from his money. And what is it now?"

"I don't know," I said, "but I have a feeling you're about to tell me."

"A fool's errand," he said. "I have two trades, burglary and bookselling. That's two sets of footprints in the sands of time, and I wouldn't encourage any son of mine to follow in either of them."

"You don't have a son," I pointed out.

"And a good thing," he said, "because what kind of a role model would I be? Two careers, and both of them victims of the Twenty-first Century."

"Oh?"

"Nobody buys books anymore," he said. "For that I blame technology, whether you call it ebooks or the Internet."

"People still steal," I said.

"And get caught, because you can't walk a block without getting your picture taken half a dozen times. There are security cameras everywhere, up and down every street and inside of most large buildings. Do you know what I did last Thursday?"

"No idea."

"Well, you would," he said, "if you looked at the right tapes. I went to an address in the East Sixties, where a supermodel whose name you would recognize uses a dresser drawer for what ought to be in a safe-deposit box."

"Jewelry?"

"Her building's a brownstone," he said, "so there's no doorman, no on-site security people. And she was in St. Croix, shooting a spread for the *Sports Illustrated* Swimsuit issue, so the house was empty."

"Except for her jewelry."

"And other valuables. I went there and I stood out in front of her building. I was close enough to see the lock on the front door, and I figured it would take me about thirty seconds to pick it. I waited while the sky darkened, and the programmed lights went on in some of the rooms." He sighed. "I had a brown paper bag in my pocket."

"To hold the loot?"

"To pull over my head. I'd already cut eye holes in the thing."

"So the cameras wouldn't trip you up."

"But what good would it do? They'd check cameras on the street, and find images of me before I put the bag over my head. Or, even if I got out of a cab with my head already in the bag, there'd be footage from the day before, when I cased the site. So I walked home."

"You walked?"

"Through Central Park. It's a pleasant route, but there may have been security cameras in the trees, taking note of my presence. If so, there's probably a picture of me taking the paper bag out of my pocket and dropping it in a trashcan."

"At least you didn't litter."

"I wouldn't dare," he said. "Not these days, in this city." In the window, his cat stretched and yawned. "Smile, Raffles," he told it. "For the camera."

THE BURGLAR
TAKES A CAT

LOOK, IT WASN'T MY idea.

And it happened very quickly. One day back in early June Carolyn brought pastrami sandwiches and celery tonic to the bookstore, and I showed her a couple of books, an Ellen Glasgow novel and the collected letters of Evelyn Waugh. She took a look at the spines and made a sound somewhere between a *tssst* and a cluck. "You know what did that," she said.

"I have a haunting suspicion."

"Mice, Bern."

"That's what I was afraid you were going to say."

"Rodents," she said. "Vermin. You can throw those books right in the garbage."

"Maybe I should keep them. Maybe they'll eat these and leave the others alone."

"Maybe you should leave a quarter under your pillow," she said, "and the Tooth Fairy'll come in the middle of the night and chew their heads off."

"That doesn't seem very realistic, Carolyn."

"No," she said. "It doesn't. Bern, you wait right here."

"Where are you going?"

"I won't be long," she said. "Don't eat my sandwich."

"I won't, but—"

"And don't leave it where the mice can get it, either."

"Mouse," I said. "There's no reason to assume there's more than one."

"Bern," she said, "take my word for it. There's no such thing as one mouse."

I might have figured out what she was up to, but I opened the Waugh volume while I knocked off the rest of my own sandwich, and one letter led to another. I was still at it when the door opened and there she was, back again. She was holding one of those little cardboard satchels with air holes, the kind shaped like a New England salt box house.

The sort of thing you carry cats in.

"Oh, no," I said.

"Bern, give me a minute, huh?"

"No."

"Bern, you've got mice. Your shop is infested with rodents. Do you know what that means?"

"It doesn't mean I'm going to be infested with cats."

"Not cats," she said. "There's no such thing as one mouse. There is such a thing as one cat. That's all I've got in here, Bern. One cat."

"That's good," I said. "You came in here with one cat, and you can leave with one cat. It makes it easy to keep track that way."

"You can't just live with the mice. They'll do thousands of dollars worth of damage. They won't sit back and settle down with one volume and read it from cover to cover, you know. No, it's a bite here and a bite there, and before you know it you're out of business."

"Don't you think you're overdoing it?"

"No way. Bern, remember the Great Library at Alexandria? One of the seven wonders of the ancient world, and then a single mouse got in there."

"I thought you said there was no such thing as a single mouse."

"Well, now there's no such thing as the Great Library at Alexandria, and all because the pharaoh's head librarian didn't have the good sense to keep a cat."

"There are other ways to get rid of mice," I said.

"Name one."

"Poison."

"Bad idea, Bern."

"What's so bad about it?"

"Forget the cruelty aspect of it."

"Okay," I said. "It's forgotten."

"Forget the horror of gobbling down something with Warfarin in it and having all your little blood vessels burst. Forget the hideous spectre of one of God's own little warmblooded creatures dying a slow agonizing death from internal bleeding. Forget all that, Bern. If you possibly can."

"All forgotten. The memory tape's a blank."

"Instead, focus on the idea of dozens of mice dying in the walls around you, where you can't see them or get at them."

"Ah, well. Out of sight, out of mind. Isn't that what they say?"

"Nobody ever said it about dead mice. You'll have a store with hundreds of them decomposing in the walls."

"Hundreds?"

"God knows the actual number. The poisoned bait's designed to draw them from all over the area. You could have mice scurrying here from miles around, mice from SoHo to Kips Bay, all of them coming here to die."

I rolled my eyes.

"Maybe I'm exaggerating a tiny bit," she allowed. "But all you need is one dead mouse in the wall and you're gonna smell a rat, Bern."

"A mouse, you mean."

"You know what I mean. And maybe your customers won't exactly cross the street to avoid walking past the store—"

"Some of them do that already."

"—but they won't be too happy spending time in a shop with a bad odor to it. They might drop in for a minute, but they won't browse. No book lover wants to stand around smelling rotting mice."

"Traps," I suggested.

"Traps? You want to set mousetraps?"

"The world will beat a path to my door."

"What kind will you get, Bern? The kind with a powerful spring, that sooner or later you screw up while you're setting it and it takes off the tip of your finger? The kind that breaks the mouse's neck, and you open up the store and there's this dead mouse with its neck broken, and you've got to deal with that first thing in the morning?"

"Maybe one of those new glue traps. Like a Roach Motel, but for mice."

"Mice check in, but they can't check out."

"That's the idea."

"Great idea. There's the poor little mousie with its feet caught, whining piteously for hours, maybe trying to gnaw off its own feet in a pathetic attempt to escape, like a fox in a leg-hold trap in one of those animal-rights commercials."

"Carolyn—"

"It could happen. Who are you to say it couldn't happen? Anyway, you come in and open the store and there's the mouse, still alive, and then what do you do? Stomp on it? Get a gun and shoot it? Fill the sink and drown it?"

"Suppose I just drop it in the garbage, trap and all."

"Now *that's* humane," she said. "Poor thing's half-suffocated in the dark for days, and then the garbage men toss the bag into the hopper and it gets ground up into mouseburger. That's terrific, Bern. While you're at it, why not drop the trap into the incinerator? Why not burn the poor creature alive?"

I remembered something. "You can release the mice from glue traps," I said. "You pour a little baby oil on their feet and it acts as a solvent for the glue. The mouse just runs off, none the worse for wear."

"None the worse for wear?"

"Well—"

"Bern," she said. "Don't you realize what you'd be doing? You'd be releasing a psychotic mouse. Either it would find its way back into the store or it would get into one of the neighboring buildings, and who's to say what it would do? Even if you let it go miles from here, even if you took it clear out to Flushing, you'd be unleashing a deranged rodent upon the unsuspecting public. Bern, forget traps. Forget poison. You don't need any of that." She tapped the side of the cat carrier. "You've got a friend," she said.

"You're not talking friends. You're talking cats."

"What have you got against cats?"

"I haven't got anything against cats. I haven't got anything against elk, either, but that doesn't mean I'm going to keep one in the store so I'll have a place to hang my hat."

"I thought you liked cats."

"They're okay."

"You're always sweet to Archie and Ubi. I figured you were fond of them."

"I *am* fond of them," I said. "I think they're fine in their place, and their place happens to be your apartment. Carolyn, believe me, I don't want a pet. I'm not the type. If I can't even keep a steady girlfriend, how can I keep a pet?"

"Pets are easier," she said with feeling. "Believe me. Anyway, this cat's not a pet."

"Then what is it?"

"An employee," she said. "A working cat. A companion animal by day, a solitary night watchman when you're gone. A loyal, faithful, hard-working servant."

"Miaow," the cat said.

We both glanced at the cat carrier, and Carolyn bent down to unfasten its clasps. "He's cooped up in there," she said.

"Don't let him out."

"Oh, come on," she said, doing just that. "We're not talking Pandora's Box here, Bern. I'm just letting him get some air."

"That's what the air holes are for."

"He needs to stretch his legs," she said, and the cat emerged and did just that, extending his front legs and stretching, then doing the same for his rear legs. You know how cats do, like they're warming up for a dance class.

"He," I said. "It's a male? Well, at least it won't be having kittens all the time."

"Absolutely not," she said. "He's guaranteed not to have kittens."

"But won't he run around peeing on things? Like books, for instance. Don't male cats make a habit of that sort of thing?"

"He's post-op, Bern."

"Poor guy."

"He doesn't know what he's missing. But he won't have kittens, and he won't father them, either, or go nuts yowling whenever there's a female cat in heat somewhere between Thirty-fourth Street and the Battery. No, he'll just do his job, guarding the store and keeping the mice down."

"And using the books for a scratching post. What's the point of getting rid of mice if the books all wind up with claw marks?"

"No claws, Bern."

"Oh."

"He doesn't really need them, since there aren't a lot of enemies to fend off in here. Or a whole lot of trees to climb."

"I guess." I looked at him. There was something strange about him, but it took me a second or two to figure it out. "Carolyn," I said, "what happened to his tail?"

"He's a Manx."

"So he was born tailless. But don't Manx cats have a sort of hopping gait, almost like a rabbit? This guy just walks around like your ordinary garden-variety cat. He doesn't look much like any Manx I ever saw."

"Well, maybe he's only part Manx."

"Which part? The tail?"

"Well—"

"What do you figure happened? Did he get it caught in a door, or did the vet get carried away? I'll tell you, Carolyn, he's been neutered and declawed and his tail's no more than a memory. When you come right down to it, there's not a whole lot of the original cat left, is there? What we've got here is the stripped-down economy model. Is there anything else missing that I don't know about?"

"No."

"Did they leave the part that knows how to use a litter box? That's going to be tons of fun, changing the litter every day. Does he at least know how to use a box?"

"Even better, Bern. He uses the toilet."

"Like Archie and Ubi?" Carolyn had trained her own cats, first by keeping their litter pan on top of the toilet seat, then by cutting a hole in it, gradually enlarging the hole and finally getting rid of the pan altogether. "Well, that's something," I said. "I don't suppose he's figured out how to flush it."

"No. And don't leave the seat up."

I sighed heavily. The animal was stalking around my store, poking his head into corners. Surgery or no surgery, I kept waiting for him to cock a leg at a shelf full of first editions. I admit it, I didn't trust the little bastard.

"I don't know about this," I said. "There must be a way to mouseproof a store like this. Maybe I should talk it over with an exterminator."

"Are you kidding? You want some weirdo skulking around the aisles, spraying toxic chemicals all over the place? Bern, you don't have to call an exterminator. You've got a live-in exterminator, your own personal organic rodent control division. He's had all his shots, he's free of fleas and ticks, and if he ever needs grooming you've got a friend in the business. What more could you ask for?"

I felt myself weakening, and I hated that. "He seems to like it here," I admitted. "He acts as though he's right at home."

"And why not? What could be more natural than a cat in a bookstore?"

"He's not bad-looking," I said. "Once you get used to the absence of a tail. And that shouldn't be too hard, given that I was already perfectly accustomed to the absence of an entire cat. What color would you say he was?"

"Gray tabby."

"It's a nice functional look," I decided. "Nothing flashy about it, but it goes with everything, doesn't it? Has he got a name?"

"Bern, you can always change it."

"Oh, I bet it's a pip."

"Well, it's not horrendous, at least I don't think it is, but he's like most cats I've known. He doesn't respond to his name. You know how Archie and Ubi are. Calling them by name is a waste of time. If I want them to come, I just run the electric can opener."

"What's his name, Carolyn."

"Raffles," she said. "But you can change it to anything you want. Feel free."

"Raffles," I said.

"If you hate it—"

"Hate it?" I stared at her. "Are you kidding? It's got to be the perfect name for him."

"How do you figure that, Bern?"

"Don't you know who Raffles was? In the books by E. W. Hornung back around the turn of the century, and in the stories Barry Perowne's been doing recently? Raffles the amateur cracksman? World-class cricket player and gentleman burglar? I can't believe you never heard of the cele-brated A. J. Raffles."

Her mouth fell open. "I never made the connection," she said. "All I could think of was like raffling off a car to raise funds for a church. But now that you mention it—"

"Raffles," I said. "The quintessential burglar of fiction. And here he is, a cat in a bookstore, and the bookstore's owned by a former burglar. I'll tell you, if I were looking for a name for the cat I couldn't possibly do better than the one he came with."

Her eyes met mine, "Bernie," she said solemnly, "it was meant to be."

"Miaow," said Raffles.

AT NOON the following day it was my turn to pick up lunch. I stopped at the falafel stand on the way to the Poodle Factory. Carolyn asked how Raffles was doing.

"He's doing fine," I said. "He drinks from his water bowl and eats out of his new blue cat dish, and I'll be damned if he doesn't use the toilet just the way you said he did. Of course I have to remember to leave the door ajar, but when I forget he reminds me by standing in front of it and yowling."

"It sounds as though it's working out."

"Oh, it's working out marvelously," I said. "Tell me something. What was his name before it was Raffles?"

"I don't follow you, Bern."

"'I don't follow you, Bern.' That was the crowning touch, wasn't it? You waited until you had me pretty well softened up, and then you tossed in the name as a sort of *coup de foie gras.* 'His name's Raffles, but you can always change it.' Where did the cat come from?"

"Didn't I tell you? A customer of mine, he's a fashion photographer, he has a really gorgeous Irish water spaniel, and he told me about a friend of his who developed asthma and was heartbroken because his allergist insisted he had to get rid of his cat."

"And then what happened?"

"Then you developed a mouse problem, so I went and picked up the cat, and—"

"No."

"No?"

I shook my head. "You're leaving something out. All I had to do was mention the word mouse and you were out of here like a cat out of hell. You didn't even have to think about it. And it couldn't have taken you more than twenty minutes to go and get the cat and stick it in a carrying case and come back with it. How did you spend those twenty minutes? Let's see—first you went back to the Poodle Factory to look up the number of your customer the fashion photographer, and then you called him and asked for the name and number of his friend with the allergies. Then I guess you called the friend and introduced yourself and arranged to meet him at his apartment and take a look at the animal, and then—"

"Stop it."

"Well?"

"The cat was at my apartment."

"What was he doing there?"

"He was living there, Bern."

I frowned. "I've met your cats," I said. "I've known them for years. I'd recognize them, with or without tails. Archie's a sable Burmese and Ubi's a Russian Blue. Neither one of them could pass for a gray tabby, except maybe in a dark alley."

"He was living *with* Archie and Ubi," she said.

"Since when?"

"Oh, just for a little while."

I thought for a moment. "Not for just a little while," I said, "because he was there long enough to learn the toilet trick. You don't learn something like that overnight. Look how long it takes with human beings. That's how he learned, right? He picked it up from your cats, didn't he?"

"I suppose so."

"And he didn't pick it up overnight, either. Did he?"

"I feel like a suspect," she said. "I feel as though I'm being grilled."

"Grilled? You ought to be char-broiled. You set me up and euchred me, for heaven's sake. How long has Raffles been living with you?"

"Two and a half months."

"Two and a half *months!*"

"Well, maybe it's more like three."

"Three months! That's unbelievable. How many times have I been over to your place in the past three months? It's got to be eight or ten at the very least. Are you telling me I looked at the cat and didn't even notice him?"

"When you came over," she said, "I used to put him in the other room."

"What other room? You live in one room."

"I put him in the closet."

"In the closet?"

"Uh-huh. So you wouldn't see him."

"But why?"

"The same reason I never mentioned him."

"Why's that? I don't get it. Were you ashamed of him? What's wrong with him, anyway?"

"There's nothing wrong with him."

"Because if there's something shameful about the animal, I don't know that I want him hanging around my store."

"There's nothing shameful about him," she said. "He's a perfectly fine cat. He's trustworthy, he's loyal, he's helpful and friendly—"

"Courteous, kind," I said. "Obedient, cheerful, thrifty. He's a regular Boy Scout, isn't he? So why the hell were you keeping him a secret from me?"

"It wasn't just you, Bern. Honest. I was keeping him a secret from everybody."

"But *why*, Carolyn?"

"I don't even want to say it."

"Come on, for God's sake."

She took a breath. "Because," she said darkly, "he was the Third Cat."

"You lost me."

"Oh, God. This is impossible to explain. Bernie, there's something you have to understand. Cats can be very dangerous for a woman."

"What are you talking about?"

"You start with one," she said, "and that's fine, no problem, nothing wrong with that. And then you get a second one and that's even better,

116

as a matter of fact, because they keep each other company. It's a curious thing, but it's actually easier to have two cats than one."

"I'll take your word for it."

"Then you get a third, and that's all right, it's still manageable, but before you know it you take in a fourth, and then you've gone and done it."

"Done what?"

"You've crossed the line."

"What line, and how have you crossed it?"

"You've become a Woman With Cats." I nodded. Light was beginning to dawn. "You know the kind of woman I mean," she went on. "They're all over the place. They don't have any friends, and they hardly ever set foot outdoors, and when they die people discover thirty or forty cats in the house. Or they're cooped up in an apartment with thirty or forty cats and the neighbors take them to court to evict them because of the filth and the smell. Or they seem perfectly normal, and then there's a fire or a break-in or something, and the world finds them out for what they are. They're Women With Cats, Bernie, and that's not what I want to be."

"No," I said, "and I can see why. But—"

"It doesn't seem to be a problem for men," she said. "There are lots of men with two cats, and probably plenty with three or four, but when did you ever hear anything about a Man With Cats? When it comes to cats, men don't seem to have trouble knowing when to stop." She frowned. "Funny, isn't it? In every other area of their lives—"

"Let's stick to cats," I suggested. "How did you happen to wind up with Raffles hanging out in your closet? And what was his name before it was Raffles?"

She shook her head. "Forget it, Bern. It was a real pussy name, if you ask me. Not right for the cat at all. As far as how I got him, well, it happened pretty much the way I said, except there were a few things I left out. George Brill is a customer of mine. I groom his Irish water spaniel."

"And his friend is allergic to cats."

"No, George is the one who's allergic. And when Felipe moved in with George, the cat had to go. The dog and cat got along fine, but George was wheezing and red-eyed all the time, so Felipe had to give up either George or the cat."

"And that was it for Raffles."

"Well, Felipe wasn't all that attached to the cat. It wasn't his cat in the first place. It was Patrick's."

"Where did Patrick come from?"

"Ireland, and he couldn't get a green card and he didn't like it here that much anyway, so when he went back home he left the cat with Felipe, because he couldn't take him through Immigration. Felipe was willing to give the cat a home, but when he and George got together, well, the cat had to go."

"And how come you were elected to take him?"

"George tricked me into it."

"What did he do, tell you the Poodle Factory was infested with mice?"

"No, he used some pretty outrageous emotional blackmail on me. Anyway, it worked. The next thing I knew I had a Third Cat."

"How did Archie and Ubi feel about it?"

"They didn't actually say anything, but their body language translated into something along the lines of, 'There goes the neighborhood.' I don't think it broke their hearts yesterday when I packed him up and took him out of there."

"But in the meantime he spent three months in your apartment and you never said a word."

"I was planning on telling you, Bern."

"When?"

"Sooner or later. But I was afraid."

"Of what I would think?"

"Not only that. Afraid of what the Third Cat signified." She heaved a sigh. "All those Women With Cats," she said. "They didn't plan on it, Bern. They got a first cat, they got a second cat, they got a third cat, and all of a sudden they were gone."

"You don't think they might have been the least bit odd to begin with?"

"No," she said. "No, I don't. Oh, once in a while, maybe, you get a slightly wacko lady, and next thing you know she's up to her armpits in cats. But most of the Cat Ladies start out normal. By the time you get to the end of the story they're nuts, all right, but having thirty or forty cats'll do that to you. It sneaks up on you, and before you know it you're over the edge."

"And the Third Cat's the charm, huh?"

"No question. Bern, there are primitive cultures that don't really have numbers, not in the sense that we do. They have a word that means 'one,' and other words for 'two' and 'three,' and after that there's a word that just means 'more than three.' And that's how it is in our culture with cats. You can have one cat, you can have two cats, you can even have three cats, but after that you've got 'more than three.'"

"And you're a Woman With Cats."

"You got it."

"I've got it, all right. I've got your third cat. Is that the real reason you never mentioned it? Because you were planning all along to palm the little bugger off on me?"

"No," she said quickly. "Swear to God, Bern. A couple of times over the years the subject of a dog or cat has come up, and you've always said you didn't want a pet. Did I ever once press you?"

"No."

"I took you at your word. It sometimes crossed my mind that you might have a better time in life if you had an animal to love, but I managed to keep it to myself. It never even occurred to me that you could use a working cat. And then when I found out about your rodent problem—"

"You knew just how to solve it."

"Well, sure. And it's a great solution, isn't it? Admit it, Bern. Didn't it do your heart good this morning to have Raffles there to greet you?"

"It was all right," I admitted. "At least he was still alive. I had visions of him lying there dead with his paws in the air, and the mice forming a great circle around his body."

"See? You're concerned about him, Bern. Before you know it you're going to fall in love with the little guy."

"Don't hold your breath. Carolyn? What was his name before it was Raffles."

"Oh, forget it. It was a stupid name."

"Tell me."

"Do I have to?" She sighed. "Well, it was Andro."

"Andrew? What's so stupid about that? Andrew Jackson, Andrew Johnson, Andrew Carnegie—they all did okay with it."

"Not Andrew, Bern. An*dro.*"

"Andrew Mellon, Andrew Gardner...*not* Andrew? Andro?"

"Right."

"What's that, Greek for Andrew?"

She shook her head. "It's short for Androgynous."

"Oh."

"The idea being that his surgery had left the cat somewhat uncertain from a sexual standpoint."

"Oh."

"Which I gather was also the case for Patrick, although I don't believe surgery had anything to do with it."

"Oh."

"I never called him 'Andro' myself," she said. "Actually, I didn't call him anything. I didn't want to give him a new name because that would mean I was leaning toward keeping him, and—"

"I understand."

"And then on the way over to the bookstore it just came to me in a flash. Raffles."

"As in raffling off a car to raise money for a church, I think you said."

"Don't hate me, Bern."

"I'll try not to."

"It's been no picnic, living a lie for the past three months. Believe me."

"I guess it'll be easier for everybody now that Raffles is out of the closet."

"I know it will. Bern, I didn't want to trick you into taking the cat."

"Of course you did."

"No, I didn't. I just wanted to make it as easy as possible for you and the cat to start off on the right foot. I knew you'd be crazy about him once you got to know him, and I thought anything I could do to get you over the first hurdle, any minor deception I might have to practice—"

"Like lying your head off."

"It was in a good cause. I had only your best interests at heart, Bern. Yours and the cat's."

"And your own."

"Well, yeah," she said, and flashed a winning smile. "But it worked out, didn't it? Bern, you've got to admit it worked out."

"We'll see," I said.

THE BURGLAR ON THE SCREEN

IF MY WORK HAS had any enduring impact on the film business, it's been as an example of unlikely casting. "You think that's crazy," someone will say, upon hearing that ChiChi the Chihuahua has been inked for the title role in *Cujo*. "How about Whoopi Goldberg playing Bernie Rhodenbarr in *Burglar?*"

Well, I can't say that's how I saw the character.

My friend Donald Westlake wrote an extended series of books about a criminal named Parker. Wonderful books, and over the years several of them were filmed. The first three actors to portray Parker were Anna Karina, Lee Marvin, and James Brown. "Parker's been played by a white man, a black man, and a woman," a friend told Don. "I think your character lacks definition."

The friend who made this observation was a writer named Joe Goldberg. No relation to Whoopi.

ODDLY, I was living in Hollywood when I first wrote about Mrs. Rhodenbarr's son Bernard. It was early 1976 and I had a one-bedroom apartment at the Magic Hotel on Highland between La Brea and Franklin. (The hotel owed its marvelous name to the Magic Castle, a private club for magicians located just up the hill to the north. I'd been there once a few years earlier as the guest of a friend, and we sat at a table where an impressively drunk practitioner of the dark arts was showing off with a deck of cards. "I'll bet you've never seen anything like this before," he said at one point, and puked onto the table with sangfroid I found enviable.)

I was broke, with no money and no prospects. I'd done nothing but write for a living since college, had in fact dropped out of college to write magazine fiction and paperback novels, and now I was 38 years old, with a couple of books written that my agent couldn't sell and a few others I'd started and couldn't finish. I'd split with my wife three years earlier, and now I owed alimony and child support. I couldn't get a job because I couldn't find one to apply for. "Man wanted to sweep up after the horses," I'd read in the want ads, and I'd figure that was something I could do. "Experience a must," it would go on, and that would kill it for me. I could tell how the interview would go. "Get the fuck out of here," the hiring boss would say, after one look at me. "You candy-ass son of a bitch, you never once swept up after a horse in your whole miserable life."

Actually, I did apply for a job. I'd left New York the previous summer, after a batch of things went wrong. We needn't dwell on them; suffice it to say that I told myself a moving target was harder to hit, and drove my rusted-out Ford station wagon down the coast to Florida and across to Los Angeles. H. L. Mencken observed somewhere that a divine hand had taken hold of the United States by the state of Maine, and lifted, with the result that everything loose wound up in Southern California.

It took me six or seven months to get there. I stopped here and there, did some writing to no discernible purpose, and kept waiting for things to get better. I stayed a month or so in Charleston, South Carolina, in an establishment on Fulton Street called *Rooms*, as that's what it said on the sign. A few blocks from *Rooms* was a cobbler's shop, and one afternoon I spotted a sign in the window, advertising the need for an apprentice.

I went in and talked with the fellow. I don't recall most of what he asked me, but I don't believe his questions could have probed too deeply. I doubt he even checked to make sure I was wearing shoes.

But I remember the last question. "Here's what I need to know," he said. "Will you stay? Because the last thing I want is to spend a couple of months training somebody and then have him take off just when he's starting to be of some use to me. So will you stick around?"

All I had to do was say yes and the job was mine, but I just couldn't do it. I admitted that I'd probably be moving on in a matter of weeks.

"Well, I appreciate your honesty," he said. "I really do. But it's a shame, because I'm a pretty decent judge of people, and I have the feeling you've got the makings of a damn good shoe-repair man."

AT THE Magic Hotel, I found myself wondering if I'd missed out on the opportunity of a lifetime. I might have found myself as a shoe-repair man, and a damn good one at that. It seemed unlikely, given that the only tool with which I'd ever been at all agile was my Smith-Corona, but who was I to question a self-acknowledged good judge of people? Suppose I'd tossed my typewriter and put down real roots at *Rooms*. We hadn't discussed salary, but my room at *Rooms* was a mere $20 a week, and I'm confident I could have negotiated a monthly rate.

Of all sad words of tongue or pen...

Never mind.

WHERE DO ideas come from? Always the beautiful question, but once in a while there's an answer.

I was, as I've mentioned, at the *Magic Hotel*. My rent, with daily maid service, was $325 a month. (Just today Trip Advisor quoted me a price of $259 a day. Even so, it would be easier to go back there than to *Rooms*; on my most recent visit to Charleston, I found a vacant lot where the place used to be. Now how could that happen in the very Mecca of Urban Preservationism?)

My quarters were comfortable, and all I really needed was a source of income. I had enough cash on hand to pay the rent for another month or two, but it wouldn't last forever. Since I couldn't even bring myself to apply for a job, I was unlikely to find one.

A little voice said, *Don't rule out crime.*

Huh?

Walk into a liquor store with a pistol, the voice continued, *and no one's gonna ask if you've done this before.*

I got the point, but the idea didn't sit well. I didn't own a pistol, or have any idea where to get one, and how would I find a liquor store where they didn't already know me? Yes, crime was a way around the *experience-a-must* requirement that kept me from sweeping up after the horses, but I was temperamentally unsuited to anything that might involve the threat of violence to another person—or, worse yet, to myself.

Burglary, said the voice. And this time it may have been a different voice. It may in fact have been mine.

A burglar could work alone. A burglar could avoid human contact, and was in fact well advised to do so. A burglar could set his own hours, creeping about by day or night, as he preferred.

It struck me that it wasn't that different from writing for a living. On the plus side, after you'd completed a bit of work, you didn't have to wait for some schmuck in a suit to give you notes on it.

On the downside, you could get arrested...

I pushed the idea away. I wasn't a criminal, for God's sake. Aside from that one time I removed the little Do-Not-Remove-This-Tag tag from the bottom of a mattress, I'd led a remarkably law-abiding life.

And what did it get you?

That voice again. Oh, what the hell, I thought, and began schooling myself in the arts of illegal entry. Specifically, I tried opening my hotel room door with a credit card. I knew that what I was trying to do was called *loiding the door,* as in celluloid, which I guess was what illegal entrants used in the days before credit cards. My AmEx card was made not of celluloid but of some sort of plastic, and it would no longer open doors in the conventional manner, having bounced the last time I tried to use it. It did in fact open the door to my room, but not without a fair amount of work on my part. And I had a feeling the doors at the *Magic Hotel* were not the last word in high-tech security.

Still, I had the feeling that I was resourceful enough to get into a house. I'd ring the bell, I'd make sure no one was home, and I'd find a way in. And I'd work quickly, and I'd avoid leaving fingerprints, and I'd limit myself to cash and jewelry, and I'd be considerate and not make a mess. And I'd get the hell out and hurry back to my hotel room, and if I'd forgotten my key I could always let myself in with my AmEx card.

Unless, of course, I managed to trigger some kind of silent alarm, and the cops caught me in the act.

So?

So? What do you mean, So?

If they catch you, they have to feed you. Think this through, will you? You've led a lawful life. You'll plead guilty and throw yourself on the mercy of the court. You're a writer, you can say you were doing research and it got out of hand. It's a first offense, they won't know about the mattress tag, so you'll probably get a suspended sentence. And who knows? It might be something for you to write about.

Oh, I thought. And went and made myself a sandwich, and was maybe three bites into it when another thought arose.

Suppose I was in somebody's bedroom, going through the dresser drawers, when the police stormed in. And suppose I threw my hands in the air, getting jewelry all over everything, prepared to go quietly and give the arresting officers no trouble. One of them would cuff me, and another would give the place a once-over, and—

And then suppose they found a dead body in another room?

Oh, said the little voice.

Oh? That's all you can say? Oh?

That would be a problem.

A problem? A *problem?* The hell you say.

That would be a book.

AND SO it would, and was. Within a day or so of this lightbulb moment, I sat down at my kitchen table and started writing. Within the week I'd completed three or four chapters, along with a couple of paragraphs of outline explaining with unwarranted confidence that Bernie Rhodenbarr would elude the police, track down the actual murderer, and win the heart of the girl, if there was one. I slapped a title on it—*Burglars Can't Be Choosers*—bundled it up and mailed it to my agent, and he sent it straight off to Random House, and they bought it.

Just like that.

My daughters flew out to spend the summer. They shared my *Magic* digs for July, and we spent August driving east. I got a little writing done in July and none in August, and after I dropped the kids with their mother in New York, I finished the book in a motel in Greenville, South Carolina.

Random House liked it, and published it in 1977. And by the time it came out I was living in New York again, in an apartment in Greenwich Village, and working on a second book about Bernie.

So you could argue that the fellow saved me from a life of crime.

SOMETHING CURIOUS happened when I began writing the book. It was coming out funny.

That wasn't the plan. The notion of being apprehended while committing one crime and winding up charged with a far more serious crime had arisen out of my own criminous fantasies. It was in fact something that I imagined happening to me, and there was nothing inherently amusing about it.

But Bernie, who waltzed past an Upper East Side doorman with a Bloomingdale's shopping bag for camouflage, insisted on being flip and sassy and loaded with attitude. And when he exits the premises, dashing off with the cops on his heels, and the doorman reflexively holds the door open for him, he calls out "I'll take care of you at Christmas!"

Hell, I thought. It's not supposed to be funny. I'll have to fix it later.

Just leave it alone, said the voice. *You idiot.*

IN 1985 my wife and I relocated to Fort Myers Beach, Florida, and that's where we were when Hollywood took an interest in Bernie Rhodenbarr. By then I'd published five books about him, four with Random House and a fifth with Arbor House. In the second, *The Burglar in the Closet*, he's your basic Urban Lonely Guy who just happens to be a burglar; he gets in trouble doing a felonious favor for his dentist. In the third book, *The Burglar Who Liked to Quote Kipling*, the series defined itself; he's become the owner of an antiquarian bookshop in Greenwich Village, and his best friend is Carolyn Kaiser, the lesbian dog-groomer with a shop two doors from his. The store and the best friend continue to feature prominently in the next two books, *The Burglar Who Studied Spinoza* and *The Burglar Who Painted Like Mondrian*—and indeed in the six books that have appeared since I resumed writing about Bernie in 1994.

But in 1985 there were just those five, and a deal came together to film *The Burglar in the Closet*. I was in Florida, my agent was in New York, and Hollywood was in Hollywood—so I only had a vague idea what was going on. I heard various names proposed for the title role, but the one that seemed most likely to all concerned was Bruce Willis, who had just emerged as the costar with Cybill Shepherd in the hit TV series, *Moonlighting*. This was well before *Die Hard* and its sequels made Willis a tough world-weary action hero; on TV he was flip and sassy and up to his ears in attitude—and thus a very sensible choice for the part of one Bernard Grimes Rhodenbarr.

And Whoopi Goldberg would be his best friend, Carolyn.

Now I don't know if they planned on keeping her a lesbian. My guess is someone figured out that her African-American heritage would be enough to limit her relationship with Bernie to one of Friends Without Benefits, but who knows? It doesn't matter, because at the ninth or tenth hour, if not quite the eleventh, Bruce Willis left the building.

I've never known what happened. Maybe Willis didn't like the deal they offered him. Maybe he got a look at the script and came to his senses. Or maybe the people in charge decided they didn't like him, or his attitude, or the way he combed his hair.

Who knows? Most deals fall apart. So? Everybody dies, but not everybody gets an autopsy. Life goes on. Movies go on. And this one needed somebody else to play the lead.

"They've decided on Whoopi," my agent told me. "No, not as Carolyn. As Bernie."

The way I heard it, it was her idea. "I can do that," she said.

And she was in the middle of a multi-picture deal, and they needed something quick to stick her in after *Jumpin' Jack Flash*, and they already had a script, sort of, so all they had to do was give it a sex-change operation.

Look, I was in Florida. We had this big old house right there on the beach. The first day I stepped out onto the sand, turned right, walked for half an hour, turned around and walked back. The second day I turned left instead, walked for half an hour, and walked back. The third day I didn't know what the hell to do with myself.

I thought about Don Westlake, and his character Parker. Maybe Bernie lacked definition. What did I know, and what was I going to do about it, and what did it matter? The picture would never get made.

Except it did.

I'VE ONLY seen it once, at a screening in a large movie house in mid-town Manhattan. I didn't like it, but that seemed almost beside the point. What I wanted was for everybody else to like it, so that it would sell a ton of tickets and generate a ton of publicity and induce people to buy a ton of books.

And while the film was running, that seemed possible. There was laughter, which is a Good Thing at a comedy. (There was also scattered laughter the one time I saw a theatrical showing of 8 *Million Ways to Die*; that picture was a far cry from a comedy, and the laughter was Not a Good Thing. It was based on my novel *Eight Million Ways to Die*, but they replaced the first word with a digit, perhaps as a cost-cutting move. Never mind.)

After the final credits rolled, our party of a dozen or so rose from our seats and headed for the exit, telling one another that we just might have a hit on our hands. That notion died in the lobby, as we heard all the strangers with whom we'd just shared this rich experience telling each other, "Well, that wasn't much good, was it?"

A few weeks later, my literary agent, Knox Burger, flew somewhere on business, and the in-flight movie was *Burglar*. Knox had been at the screening, and so paid less attention to what was on the screen than to the reactions of his seat mate. The fellow, an MBA in his thirties, laughed throughout, and when he sat back and took off his ear phones, Knox asked him how he'd enjoyed the film.

"It wasn't much good," the guy said.

Knox, incredulous, pointed out that he'd been laughing.

"Oh, there are some funny bits," the fellow allowed. "They give you a couple of laughs. But there's never a moment when you lose sight of the fact that what you're watching is crap."

IT WOULD be very easy to blame Whoopi.

I don't, and never did. She was playing an ill-conceived role in a doomed film with a lousy script, and it always seemed to me that she did the best she could with what they handed her. (Full disclosure: I'm saying this on the basis of that initial screening. I've only seen *Burglar* once, and that's okay. I did see *8 Million Ways to Die* a second time, on a surreal afternoon when Lynne and I, slogging on foot across northern Spain on our way to Santiago de Compostela, finished the day in a hotel bar somewhere in Navarre. We collapsed, way beyond exhaustion, and the waiter brought us cheese sandwiches and café con leche, and we looked up, and there on the television set were Jeff Bridges and Andy Garcia, their voices dubbed in Spanish. It took us a good ten minutes to be sure we weren't hallucinating.)

The critics didn't like *Burglar*. Roger Ebert had this to say:

"Does Hollywood think Whoopi Goldberg recently arrived here from another planet? Do they think she has one of those invisible protective shields around her, like in the old toothpaste commercials? Do they respond at all to her warmth, her energy, her charisma? Sure, she looks a little funny, but why isn't she allowed to have normal relationships in the movies? Why is she always packaged as the weirdo from Planet X? The occasion for these questions is "Burglar," a witless, hapless exercise in the wrong way to package Goldberg. This is a woman who is original. Who is talented. Who has a special relationship with the motion picture comedy. It is criminal to put her into brain-damaged, assembly-line thrillers."

SO I don't blame Whoopi, and neither do I blame the decision to cast her in the role. While it's unarguably true that Bernie Rhodenbarr as I envisioned him was neither black nor female, well, so what? I can't really sell myself on the notion that a filmmaker's primary aim ought to be the transference of the author's vision to the screen. Fans of my books might indeed be happier with a film whose lead character was closer to their image of Bernie, but if all my readers saw the film several times over, that wouldn't put enough asses in enough seats to make the movie turn a profit. For that to happen, *Burglar* would have to sell a good deal more tickets than I sold books, and it would have to sell them to people who'd be meeting Bernie Rhodenbarr for the first time.

I could point to aspects of the film I didn't like—the writing, the direction—but so could everybody else, and with as much validity. I had a personal aversion to Bobcat Goldthwait, whose impersonation of a nervous breakdown I always find cringe-inducing, but he didn't kill the movie. It would have been every bit as dead with someone else playing Carolyn.

So who's to blame?

My fucking agent.

NOT FOR the film. I'm not sorry the film was made, and why should I be? It helped me pay for my house, the one I mentioned, the one right on the beach in Florida. It was a happy day when we paid off that mortgage, though not nearly as happy as the day a couple of years later when we sold the place and moved back to New York.

Burglar didn't sell any books, not really, but in 1994 I resumed writing about Bernie, and when I went on tour for *The Burglar Who Traded Ted Williams*, it gave me something to talk about. It was a rare appearance that someone didn't bring it up.

And it was also a rare year that went by without someone wanting to make another Bernie Rhodenbarr movie—with more conventional casting, too. But Knox Burger, who negotiated the deal for *Burglar* himself rather than partnering with a film agent, managed to sign away the rights to all the books forever. My current Hollywood agent, looking to see if there was a way out, read the contract I'd signed and pronounced it the worst one he'd ever seen. If anyone ever wants to make a movie about Bernie, they have to get Warners to sign off—and lots of luck with that.

Oh, let it go. Knox is gone now, and I liked him, and he was a good agent in many respects. And *de mortuis* and all that, you know?

And, as time passes, I find myself reluctant to pass judgment on any motion picture. I think of Dr. Johnson, likening a woman preaching to a dog walking on its hind legs. It is not done well, he told Boswell, but you are surprised to find it done at all.

That a picture actually gets made is remarkable enough. Pointing out that it's not much good seems, well, picky.

A BURGLAR'S FUTURE

I THOUGHT I WAS just going out for a walk, doing what I could to pacify my Fitbit, but wouldn't you know it? My feet had ideas of their own, and in no time at all they'd led me to that block of East Eleventh Street between University Place and Broadway.

A tailless cat sunned itself in the window of Barnegat Books, and barely stirred when I opened the door. I got a slightly warmer reception from my favorite bookseller, who was perched on his stool behind the counter. He looked up from his book, said "Oh, it's you," and resumed reading.

"It's me," I agreed.

A quick look around established that the proprietor and his cat and I had the store to ourselves, unless you count the spirits of a few thousand dead writers. "Good to see you," I said. "Um, how's business?"

"Don't ask."

"All right."

He sighed, and answered the question now that I'd withdrawn it. "Business," he said, "is non-existent. I'm essentially out of business. You know the bargain table I keep out front?"

"I knew something was missing," I said. "What happened to it? Don't tell me somebody walked off with it."

"If only," he said with feeling. "It was rare enough that someone swiped a book. No, I got tired of hauling it out every morning and bringing it in every night. And I got tired of people bringing a book inside and buying it and then cluttering up the store browsing through books they'd go home and order on line."

"Oh," I said.

"The world's a different place," he said. "Barnegat Books was already an anachronism when I bought it. Still, people used to read. They used to collect first editions, and track down the complete works of writers they discovered. Now they zone out with Netflix, and what reading they do is on an eReader or an iPad. And if they're old-fashioned enough to collect books, they don't have to hunt for them. Why breathe in the dust of an old bookshop when you can find anything you could possibly want through a five-minute online search?"

"You make it sound awful."

"But it's not," he said. "It's just different. Unless you have a store like this one, in which case the answer is obvious."

"Oh?"

He nodded. "Close up shop," he said. "You know, I never expected to make money here. I figured if I could break even, or keep losses to a minimum, I'd have a place to hang out and sponsor poetry readings and, well—"

"Meet girls?"

"And I met a few," he allowed, "and sometimes that was good and sometimes it wasn't, like life itself. And there was another benefit of owning the place. I had this other occupation."

"Burglary."

He nodded. "And I made enough at night to cover any losses I incurred day-to-day. But now that the entire planet's wired for closed circuit TV, with security cameras everywhere you can imagine and some places you can't, well, forget it. There's no cash anywhere anyhow, and if you steal something nobody's going to buy it from you, and being a burglar makes even less sense than being a bookseller. Two occupations, one legit and one not, and both of them rendered obsolete by encroaching technology."

"You sound as though you're getting ready to close the store."

He looked at me. "And then what would I do? This city's extortionate rent increases would have forced me out of here twenty years ago if I hadn't been able to buy the building. This way I make enough renting out the apartments upstairs to keep body and soul together. If I had any sense I'd close this money pit, truck all these goddamn books to a landfill, and rent out the store to a chain drugstore or a boutique. You know what I could get for this space?"

"A good deal, I suppose."

"As far as that goes," he said, "I could sell the whole building. Get a few million for it. Retire somewhere. But you know what the problem is, don't you?"

"You're too young to retire."

He glared at me. "And I always will be," he said, "thanks to you, you son of a bitch. Back in 1977 I was around 35 years old. Now it's what, 2019?"

"Last I looked."

"And I'm still around 35 years old. The other guy you write about ages in real time. Matthew Fucking Scudder, the sonofabitch gets a year older with every passing year. Me, I stay the same year after year, frozen in time."

"So does Carolyn."

"Well, thank God for that. She stays the same, and so does the fucking cat. Raffles came to work here in 1994. That's what, 25 years ago? And he was a year or two old at the time. So he's gotta be 26 or 27, and do you have any idea what that is in dog years?"

"Dog years?"

"You know what I mean. He's almost as old as those Thai yowlers Lillian Jackson Braun wrote about. One of them was named Koko, and the other wasn't."

"Or maybe it was the other way around."

He gave me a look. "Now Raffles is establishing himself as The Cat Who Lived Forever."

"Well—"

"Never mind," he said. "I'm not about to sell the building. I'm not closing the store, either, and I'm not moving anywhere. I'll just stay here."

"Actually," I said, "I have to admit I'm glad to hear that. You know, people ask me about you all the time."

He rolled his eyes. "When are you gonna write another book about me. That's what they ask, right?"

"All the time."

"Tell them," he said, "never."

"That seems so final."

"Good."

"They keep coming up with suggestions," I said. "Things for you to steal. Just the other day a guy wrote that his girlfriend is a violinist, and she'd had a chance to play on a Stradivarius or some other priceless violin, and he thought of Katie Huang and wondered if there was some sort of priceless flute you could steal for her, or something."

"Katie Huang," he said.

"The Taiwanese flautist who worked at Two Guys."

"I know who she is," he said. "Haven't seen her lately. And the restaurant changed hands. Two Guys from Taichung is now Two Guys from Dushanbe. That's in Tajikistan."

"Oh."

"And it's not a terrible idea, but you know as well as I do that something to steal isn't an idea for a book. It's just something to steal, and to hell with stealing."

"Point taken. Another guy emailed to tell me how he'd walked into a high-security building the other day completely by accident. He'd been a responsible citizen and picked up an armload of trash in the street, and he couldn't find a trashcan, and he walked to a building entrance to ask the doorman where he could find a trash receptacle, but the doorman wasn't paying much attention, and some tenant saw him with his arms full and held the door for him, and before he knew it he was inside this secure building."

He looked almost interested. "So what did he steal?" he wondered.

"Nothing."

"Nothing?"

"He found a trash can, and got rid of what he was holding, and turned around and got out of there."

"Hell of a story," he said. "Alert the media!"

"Well, *he* thought it was interesting. And I'd have to agree, especially in this age of security cameras."

"And you want to write a story about it?"

"Well, no," I admitted.

"Is there anything you want to write a story about? Really?"

"Um—"

"Suppose I was still up for having adventures. Suppose I was as young at heart as I am in years. Suppose the two of us put our heads together and came up with something that would work, something you haven't already written before, something genuinely good."

I waited.

"Tell me the truth," he said. "Would you be up for writing it?"

"I guess not."

"Because you've aged in real time," he said.

I nodded. "It's the biggest mistake I ever made."

"Well, it's a problem," he agreed, "but I'm here to tell you that staying the same age forever isn't so hot either. If I'm too young to retire, well, you're way past retirement age. I read your latest novella, the one where Matt Scudder's every bit as old as you are."

"*A Time to Scatter Stones.*"

"A novella instead of a full-length novel. I'm guessing neither one of you had the energy for a longer book. I liked it, but it felt like a swan song."

"It probably was."

"And you've been doing anthologies. I read one of them. They've been well-received."

"I get good writers," I said, "and stay out of their way."

"Will there be more of them?"

"I don't know," I admitted. "They're a lot of work. I'm beginning to think maybe enough is enough."

"Amen to that. So what'll you do?"

I shrugged. "Walk enough to keep my Fitbit happy. Hang out with my wife. Watch a little TV, maybe travel a little. You?"

"Sit right here," he said. "God knows I won't run out of things to read. Have lunch with Carolyn, grab drinks after work at the Bum Rap. As long as my upstairs tenants keep paying their rent, I can afford to keep the store open. Even if nobody ever comes in and buys something."

"I'm glad of that," I told him. "The place suits you."

"I guess."

"And I like having it here. You know, so I can drop by every once in a while for a little company and conversation. I enjoy our talks."

"Come over any time," he said. "God knows I'm not going anywhere."